Rose Street Revisited

Carmen J. Leone

Calcagni & Associates

Youngstown, Ohio 2000

Rose Street Revisited

ISBN 0-936369-48-5
Copyright © 2000
by Carmen John Leone

Calcagni and Associates
5922 South Avenue, Suite C
Boardman, OH 44512
(330) 965-9765
(330) 758-0014 fax
e-mail:
racalcag@gateway.net
or
cjleone@hotmail.com

Credits: The following appeared earlier in Buon Giorno Magazine: "This Gift," "Commare Josephine," "Rose Street Christmas," "Our Own Personal Crow," "State Zitto Mangiate," and "Buona Sera: To Danny."

Published in the United States of America
Youngstown, Ohio

All Rights Reserved

For all our Rose Street family and friends, who knew what it meant to love, and for all our children and theirs, those who try to live now in the spirit of those early times and places.

Preface

The reception of *Rose Street: A Family Story* prompted me to write more on the subject. The truth is that I was working against a deadline with that book: Cousin Bob Calcagni and I wanted to present it as a Christmas gift to our family in 1996, so I had to stop the writing in a reasonable enough time to get it bound for the holiday. The main story was finished anyway, and perhaps in the novel format that I used any additional "stories" would have been inappropriate there. However, I had more to say about those folks and those days. This is my attempt to say more.

As with *Rose Street,* the stories here are as historically accurate as I could make them, though in dramatizing them I had to use my imagination. They are all *true*.

Hope you enjoy them as well as the poems, sketches, photos and other documents through which I try to elicit the spirit of the times.

All of the poems were written long after Rose Street, and few of them were written with Rose Street in mind, but they are included because, I think, the spirit is there.

And please try the recipes, even though their brevity leaves lots of room for error.

Table of Contents

Memories of Rose Street 1

This Gift 6

Commare Josephine 7

For Teresa 10

Rose Street Christmas 11

My Uncle Joe 18

Reversal: To Chris 21

On the Kitchen Table 22

Looking For Something Lost 27

The Three First Mysteries 28

Toots and the Attic Ghost 29

He Was Only Three 37

Our Own Personal Crow 38

Pepper Passes 46

A Sonnet for My Son 48

The Wilson 51

Christopher, David, and Danny, and Gene
.... 56

State Zitto e Mangiate 58

Dom 68

To Andi 69

Guitar Blues 71

A Little White Square with Black Spots . 83

Transformation 99

To My Father 100

Gently Strumming 101

Riddle 103

The Garland Girls 104

Love Notes From Teresa 110

Four Americanos and a French Bride ... 112

Buona Sera: To Danny 122

DOCUMENTS 124

Memories of Rose Street

My memories of Rose Street are a little different from those of some of the earlier neighbors, since I didn't arrive until halfway through the family's stay there. We moved from Rose when I was twelve, so I have only about ten years of memory from there to call on, and much of it has become muddled with age. I don't know how much of what I have stored about this street of my birth and of my roots is fact and how much is legend, which is at least truth if not fact.

Not that my Rose Street didn't exist. There are still many among family and old neighbors who can corroborate my account. But from our perspective, decades later, it's like a miracle that it ever happened, another world where we were at home and comfortable and, above all, innocent; a kind of second womb that we've burst from, into a darker, less friendly world.

My generation was born there, crying out our first bawls from its houses. Our mothers and fathers had been born and most of them raised in poor Italian villages. It was a New World for them as well as us. We and they approached it with awe. They approached it with a good deal of faith in Divine Providence, and that rubbed off on most of us.

Maybe that's what made our neighborhood so special. We were poor, but we were either unaware of it or we simply accepted it. We had adequate, clean shelter and all the food we needed.

Rose Street Revisited

Much of our food was grown in small back yards under the tender care of our fathers and prepared in small kitchens, lovingly, by our mothers.

All of the mothers and fathers, the Italian immigrants, are gone now. Some of their children, those of my generation, are also gone. Among those still living I occasionally see someone, usually at a wake, or perhaps in a grocery store. We stop and talk. The conversation generally winds its way to the topic of Rose Street. I see a certain sparkle in their eyes and I'm sure they see it in mine. Our thoughts are on a Paradise Lost. It's not despair over the loss that most comes across to me. Rather it's a kind of thankfulness that we at least had something special for a while, a chance in this life to get a taste of what's in store for us in the next.

From Rose we could walk wherever we wanted to go. Sometimes, though, the things I remember came to us. It was an age and ours was a neighborhood for street vendors and traveling salesmen and hucksters: There was the rags man, an old ragged man himself, with a strange, dirty, black felt hat, who came around with his horse and wagon calling out, "Rags! Bones! Iron!" What he did with this trash that he paid us pennies for I could never figure out.

There was the jolly, mustached popcorn man, who came around on foot wheeling his bright, flaming machine, sending the heavenly aroma of hot buttered popcorn and roasted peanuts over the neighborhood. As I recall him, he came at night, in the dark, the glow from his fire lighting up his happy face.

Rose Street Christmas

A face I often confuse with this popcorn man's in my early memory is that of the organ grinder. This jolly, brightly dressed man traveled through the neighborhoods with his monkey, which was attired, in my memory, like the Philip Morris bellhop. While the old man ground out his melodies, the monkey danced and passed his hat for our coins of appreciation.

Speaking of grinders, there was the man we called the scissors grinder, who traveled the streets, also on foot, wheeling his cart and grindstone to sharpen knives and scissors.

And there was the vendor of shaved ice, who could transform the simple block of ice into a sweet, cool refreshment that we ate and drank at the same time.

A neighborhood favorite was Louie the Iceman—Louis Vigliotti. He came daily from his icehouse in his truck, moving slowly along the street, singing out in his deep voice, "Ice-a frisca, ice-a frisca." He was a huge, strong man, and he picked up great blocks of ice with his tongs and shouldered them to the Rose Street iceboxes. We had cards with numbers representing the amount of ice we needed that day. We placed them on the doorknob for Louie to see.

There was also the coal man. We all used coal furnaces for heating in those days. The truck backed up to the coal cellar "window" and the coal rolled down the chute in a cloud of heavy black dust.

Others did frequent business in our neighborhood. The insurance man, Mr. Pape, came around at regular intervals to collect life insurance

Rose Street Revisited

premiums. A man from the Sweetheart Soap Company brought cases of laundry and bar soap. Our most regular "suit and tie" visitor was a gentleman named Tony, who came daily to pick up the lottery slips. Although the "bug," as we called it, was illegal in those days, almost every household on Rose Street invested pennies and nickels and dimes and sometimes even quarters and half-dollars. One of my sister Dolores's jobs every weekday evening was to write out Pop's numbers in his "bug book" for the next day's pick-up.

    Back then I was too young to recognize all the darker things that were surely going on in the world, even in this small world of Rose Street. Now I am too old to remember them. Either perspective is satisfying.

Cranberry Salad

1 large Pkg of Black cherry Jello
2 cup water boiling
1 cup sugar
    chopped
2 cup cranberry
1 c nuts
1 c celery
½ c Pineapple juice put water
1 c can crushed Pineapple
mixe together and let
stand in ice Box

This Gift

My father,
Sparkling eyes,
Tired from long day's work,
But sparkling.
Opening the crates with him,
dumping,
turning,
feeling as we turn the pop,
the sudden bursts,
the flow of juices,
purpling us.
Crushing,
pressing,
singing drop by drop,
stream by stream by drop,
by drip,
by drip.
Then nothing but the smell and sight
of sweetly bubbling
bubbling sweet and sticky,
blue and sweet and blinking,
bursting blue.

And papa dreams aloud
of when he was a child
and danced on grapes to make them
        burst,
and sang and swirled and laughed,
as he laughs now and sings.

This gift he gave to me.

Commare Josephine

On Sundays after the noon Mass at the Italian church, new babies were presented for baptism. In those days, the godparents—the *compares* and *commares*—brought the babies to church, usually with the babies' fathers. The mother generally did not attend, because, as the rules had it in those days, she had to be "churched" after having a baby before she resumed participation in the church's activities. This "churching" involved the priest saying certain prayers over the new mother, a ritual that took place at the Communion rail before the baptism if the mother attended. But, as I said, she usually didn't. She was home, probably preparing the Sunday dinner, which on this occasion would also be a baptismal celebration.

On one particular Sunday, Jo was among those waiting after Mass had let out for Father Franco to officiate over the baptism. He had ceremoniously removed his vestments in the sacristy and ambled next door where his Sunday dinner awaited him. The six babies and their godparents and fathers would have to wait for his return. The men quickly dispersed to the church steps for cigars while the women held their godchildren in the vestibule, trying to keep the babies comfortable.

This day Father Franco was unusually long about his dinner, or so it seemed to the ladies, for the babies fussed, and one fussy baby begat another, until the vestibule rang with infant howls. The commares did their best to comfort the little ones, but they continued their protests.

It happened that Jo was a nursing mother herself, so she instinctively put the child in her arms to her breast. In moments it was asleep, in spite of the din that surrounded them. Without a word she offered to trade babies with the young lady that stood next to her trying to comfort a wailing child. Soon this child was fast asleep also. Another *commare* presented her charge to Josephine, who gently put this third child to her breast with the same calming result. Before long, each of the babies, red and screaming, had been passed to Josephine, and each was returned to its proper *commare* in a peaceful sleep.

When the tardy priest appeared at the side door and shuffled down the aisle to the vestibule, his approach was greeted with a fitting silence from ladies and babies alike.

*****

Years later, when Mama told this story to us, she told it on herself more than about herself. The world had changed enough that she wondered at her own boldness and lack of concern for hygiene in her solution to the wailing baby problem. "Mothers today would 'have a fit,'" as she put it, at the thought of their babies being passed along for feeding without any thought of sterilizing the source of their nourishment.

But this was Josephine. I don't think any story sums her up as well as this one.

For Teresa

If I had but the grace a-
n artist needs to trace a
face upon a place a-
ssigned to tracing faces
      full of grace,
the face I'd trace u-
pon the place and
not erase a
tiny trace of
would be the face of
Teresa.

Rose Street Christmas

Each year it began when Mama and Aunt Mary walked Junior and Dolores and Aunt Mary's little girl, Georgie, downtown to look at the magic in the big windows at Strouss's and at McKelvey's. Sometimes Junior's cousins, Sonny and Angelo, came too. They and Dolores were older than Junior, but he was more than a year older than Georgie.

McKelvey's window was bigger and had more Christmas stuff in it than Strouss's. But Junior knew Strouss's better. Mama and Aunt Mary took them there more often, so he felt at home there. Aunt Mary called it *Zizi Strouss,* which meant "Uncle Strouss," because they spent all their money there. They always went down to the bargain basement and had a Frosted Malted, and Mama bought their shoes in the shoe department in the basement, where they were cheaper and they had that machine where you stuck your foot in and it showed you all your foot bones and toe bones so you could see how the new shoe fit and didn't have to just go on how it felt. All the cheaper things were in the basement, so that's where they usually shopped, but sometimes they got to ride the elevator to the top floors where the girl called out what they sold on each floor and their stomachs felt funny, like on the rides at Idora Park. And then the store got escalators and he and Dolores and Georgie rode up and down on them while Mama and Aunt Mary shopped. That's why he felt so much better about Strouss's and always wanted them to have a better Christmas window than McKelvey's.

But they almost never did. He and Dolores and his cousins voted on it every year and McKelvey's always won. Their bigger window could fit more things in it. There was Santa Claus, usually watching his elves make toys and laughing while he watched. The elves were busy moving back and forth, picking things up and putting them down and showing them to Santa Claus. Mrs. Claus and some reindeer were always there. And of course toys and games. All kinds of toys. Big, small, moving, not moving. There was an electric train, either a Lionel or an American Flyer, with all kinds of switches and cars and bridges and roads and mountains and houses and a fancy train station. On the speakers outside you could hear Santa Claus talking between "Ho ho's" to the elves or his wife or the reindeer and watching over them. Everyone was busy and safe and happy. It was magic.

Every year it was different at both stores but still pretty much the same. Junior knew it was impossible, so he never asked for any of the things in the windows. Just to see them was enough.

It was the beginning of the greatest time of the year. The time that made the cold weather and even school worth it.

Besides the windows there was the day Santa Claus came to town in an airplane at Bernard's Airport. This happened right after Thanksgiving, somewhere around the same time as the windows. That year, when Junior was eight, Papa drove them in his '31 Chevy and dropped them off with Aunt Mary. Aunt Mary told them to stay right with her so they wouldn't get lost in the crowd. But when they heard the plane and all the kids shouting they couldn't wait. When the plane landed they were supposed to stay behind the rope and wait for Santa Claus to get out with the pilot so they could wave to him. But all the yelling kids started running to the plane when it stopped. He and Georgie were short enough to fit right under the rope and they ran too. They got pushed along with the crowd of bigger kids. Junior didn't care anymore about Santa Claus because he didn't know where Aunt Mary was, or his sister and other cousins.

Georgie cried. Junior tried not to because he was older. But they got pushed and shoved by the bigger kids and they couldn't see anything but the sky over head above the bigger kids pushing them and stepping on them. Georgie screamed and Junior tried to hold her but he was crying too. Then there was Angelo putting his arm on his shoulder and yelling "They're here!" and telling them they're going to get it for running and getting lost. Then Aunt Mary was there with Dolores and Sonny.

Aunt Mary took their hands, one on each side. She looked mad but she didn't say anything. She just walked them through the crowd with his sister and cousins away from wherever Santa Claus was, out to the parking lot to wait for Papa to come back and pick them up.

Junior felt ashamed for ruining everybody's day because he was older than Georgie and should have known better, but he had run too. His sister and cousins were mad at him, but Aunt Mary didn't even holler. He wasn't worried about Papa because Papa wouldn't say anything. He'd just let Mama yell at him. But Aunt Mary didn't even tell on him when Papa came, and she probably never told Mama because Mama never yelled at him about it. But he felt bad about ruining the fun for his sister and cousins and for himself. This would be a bad memory about Christmas that he would always have.

But even it wasn't so bad because they got found and Aunt Mary didn't tell and Santa Claus brought him stuff anyway when Christmas Eve came.

But Junior worried about something for the first time that year. If Santa Claus came in on an airplane right after Thanksgiving, what was he doing in Youngstown for almost a month before Christmas when he was supposed to be up at the North Pole rushing to get all the toys made? And what about the reindeer? How could he come to town a month early in an airplane and then come again in a sleigh with reindeer?

And what was he doing in Youngstown anyway? What about the rest of the world?

At night in bed Junior tried to figure it out. He knew his mother and father couldn't be lying to him about Santa Claus because for one thing they would never lie and for another thing everybody else in the whole world knew about Santa Claus. Could they all be fooled? Was it a trick on everybody? He wanted to ask Mama, but he was afraid of what the answer might be. Maybe it wasn't supposed to make sense.

Just like the Easter Bunny didn't make any sense at all. Even less than Santa Claus. But he knew there really was an Easter Bunny because

Angelo told him he saw it last Easter when he heard a noise and jumped out of bed and looked out the window and saw it running across his yard.

Then on Christmas Eve, after the supper with all the fish, one of the grown ups heard the sleigh bells and told them to listen. Then they went to the door and Santa Claus was there—they didn't have a fireplace for him to come down—with a white bag and a whole lot of other bags on the porch, some of which said Strouss' and McKelvey's and were full of presents and stuff. And Santa Claus sat on a big chair not saying anything. Just ringing a bell. And they took turns sitting on his lap. When Junior sat on his lap he took a close look at Santa Claus. His beard looked a lot like cotton and his eyes looked like Aunt Mary's. But he wouldn't let himself look around the room for Aunt Mary. He didn't want to *not* see her. He didn't want to know about the airplane and the reindeer and the porch filled with bags that said Strouss' and McKelvey's.

There were a lot of things he didn't want to know about. Everyone around him in the room was happy and he had to be happy too.

He *was* happy. He tried to tell himself that there were two worlds. The world that made sense but wasn't always fun and the world where everybody was happy. He wanted to live in that second world with Mama and Papa and all of his family around him. Where they ate great Christmas food—smelts and devil fish and artichokes and macaroni and honey drops, and the next day wedding soup and veal cutlets and stuffed olives and more macaroni—and drank pop and laughed together.

15

Where they sang with Uncle Dom and Queenie and his guitar and went over to the church that was all decorated in beautiful colors and lights and had Mass and sang Christmas carols. Where it snowed on you when you walked home through Conti's path, and Mama let you stay up as long as you wanted. Where Papa had a glass of wine with Uncle Nick, and the food and cookies were still on the table, and Uncle Nick passed out chocolate money and played *morra* with them, and he and Georgie and Dolores tried out their new games. Where there were so many things to do, and everybody was busy and everybody was safe and everybody was happy. Just like inside that magic Christmas window at Strouss's and at McKelvey's.

Grandma's Lemon

4 C. flour
3/4 C. sugar
6 eggs
1/2 C. oil
2 tbsp. B. Powder
pinch salt

roll, cut and Bake
5 minutes
Ice with lemon
flavor.

Rose Street Revisited

My Uncle Joe

The pretty nurse floats in.
A Pepsodent smile lights her to his teeth in the
tray on
          the bed stand.
The teeth disappear
and she floats out again.

Pop and I look down upon his brother's form
          wrapped tight in white,
right arm, left foot shackled to his bed.
From the top, where his wrinkled, deep-tanned
head
          protrudes,
his eyes speak fear,
but from his mouth roll out Italian sounds,
music, though hoarse and barely audible.
They tell me only that he is awake
and trying to come back to us.

My father, across the bed from me, stoops close,
Then looks across and stuns me with Italian.
"I don't know what you say, Pop," I smile back.
"I don't know what *he* says," he translates.

In again floats the nurse,
Pepsodent smile in her head,
another in her hand.
This she drops into the hole in the tanned head,
with a "There now. Isn't that better?"
My uncle smiles and mumbles on,

My Uncle Joe

as she drops back and out the door again,
smiling always on her way.
Only slightly clearer are his sounds, the words still
    meaningless.
It's something about his garden, that much I can
tell.

"Don't worry. We take care of it," my father says,
and I silently resolve to see every one of his
tomato plants to its maturity—
if I have to.

There's nothing else that I can do for him.
I cannot even talk to him.
Now he seems to know no English,
and I never did know Italian.

Reversal: To Chris

I sit, my son, and watch you at your work.
As you stand in your winter working garb,
ax poised to strike, it's very clear to me
you've never been a chip off my old block.
I never got adjusted to that work
and couldn't hit the mark if I was paid.
The ax descends and four symmetric logs
fall like a flower's petals opening.

That sudden joy of blended cold and heat
was never in my face when I was young.
I never liked the cold and was content
to sit and watch, from inside looking out,
as I do now, at other people's work.
A pencil was more comforting to me
than axes, hammers, wrenches, spades, or nails.

I guess I don't see me in you at all.
But I don't mind. That's just the way it is.
I'm sure my father thought the same of me,
for he was always handy, just like you.

Just yesterday as I walked by your room
disgruntled—over what I don't recall—
you stood beside your door and asked me in
and gave me candy from your Christmas sock
and chided me for being so upset
and smiled and offered me another piece,
just as my father would have done for me.

Another perfect strike. You look and smile
and I am pleased and ease myself to sleep.

Rose Street Revisited

On the Kitchen Table

It seems to me that the kitchen table doesn't get the respect it deserves in families today. Other home contents seem more important. The refrigerator stores and preserves our nourishment. The bed gives us rest and has its role in perpetuating the family. The TV, stereo, and computer entertain us and give us information. The washer and dryer keep our clothes clean while the bathroom fixtures keep our bodies clean. As tables go, it's the lace-covered dining room table that shows us off to our guests and to ourselves on Sundays and other special days. But the kitchen table? Not much respect.

Sure we eat there more often than anywhere else in the house. But in these hurried and harried days we often grab our food individually and on the run, using the table only as the place to set the coffee cup or lay out the sandwich items. Or it becomes the dumping area for things we don't know what to do with: the schoolbooks, the new and old mail, the laundry waiting to be folded, the notes we leave to each other (though in most homes the refrigerator door has pretty much taken over that job).

My own memories of the kitchen table place it at the center of our family life. When I was a child it wasn't much to look at, just a sturdy, rectangular, wooden structure with a scratched surface that was sometimes covered with a cloth, more often not. It stood in the center of our kitchen, which in an Italian home was pretty much where it all happened. On weekdays and Saturdays we ate

On the Kitchen Table

every meal here, always at a regular time, with all the family that could possibly be gathered around. I see that table bearing cooling loaves of Mama's homemade bread. I see and catch the delicious aroma of chunked or sliced provolone, salami, and pepperoni. I see the sugar bowl and the milk bottle, the butter dish and knife, the "mapina"—our dialect name for the damp towel we shared in place of napkins—and often a bottle of Papa's homemade wine. Sometimes strips of flattened macaroni dough cover the entire surface of the table awaiting the "chitarra" wires to transform it to spaghetti. If it is September the whole house, but especially the kitchen, is pungent with tomatoes bubbling on the stove, their steam dampening a table laden with canning jars and lids.

When we weren't eating, when food was the last thing on our minds, though we picked and nibbled at it constantly, the table was our meeting place. Here neighbors shared coffee and gossip. Here family, one-on-one or the whole clan, aired problems, pleaded, argued, laughed, and sometimes cried to be understood. Here we played cards and here we prayed. On some evenings when Mama had a special, urgent request of God we prayed around the table, on our knees, reciting the rosary.

Then I grew to manhood and eventually presided at my own table with my own children. At first our kitchen table was much the same as in my youth, minus the rosary recitations. But as the family grew and my generation's sense of democracy took charge, we replaced our traditional rectangular table with a round one, a huge Camelot of a table, eight feet in diameter, where we were each equally placed and had an equal voice in eating and other family matters. (That's what I told the kids anyway.)

We resolved the problems of wasted space in the middle of such a large table and of having to pass everything around the great circumference by adding a very large lazy Susan, four feet in diameter, with two smaller Susans atop the base to make it possible to reach items even at the very center. We each got our food faster that way without having to bother anyone else. There was now no need to say "Please pass" anything. All courtesy ended. It was just spin and grab, spin and grab. Every now and then someone spun while someone else grabbed and was left holding the serving fork while the spaghetti flew away. But it worked pretty well, in the "fast food" spirit of the day.

In the beginning we said Grace instinctively. As time passed it became an afterthought along with the family prayers at the end of the meal.

In the beginning the table was the site of the family forum. Everyone was there. All of the day's problems were aired and often resolved. Then, so slowly that we hardly saw it happen, the gathering shrunk. Who had to stay after school for play practice, who had a Little League game, who had to work....

After a time, if the lazy Susan had been our table it would have been large enough. The prayers stopped. The discussions stopped. Even the food, after a time, more or less stopped. It was every man for himself, grabbing a bite on the way in or out.

On the Kitchen Table

Who needed a table to sit at? Today the kids are gone, off on their own. The round table leans in the barn loft, replaced by a table that looks much like the one I remember in my childhood. Seldom is there actually food on it. Still, as often as I can, on Sunday I call the kids together—those who are still in town. We avoid the dining room. We sit at the kitchen table and twirl our pasta (we don't call it macaroni now!). We sometimes even remember to say Grace. We eat and talk and eat and talk. Life is once again as it should be. I raise my wineglass and offer a *buona salude* to this simple altar of my youth. The kids echo my *salude*—partly, I think, to humor me, but partly, I hope, because they understand.

25

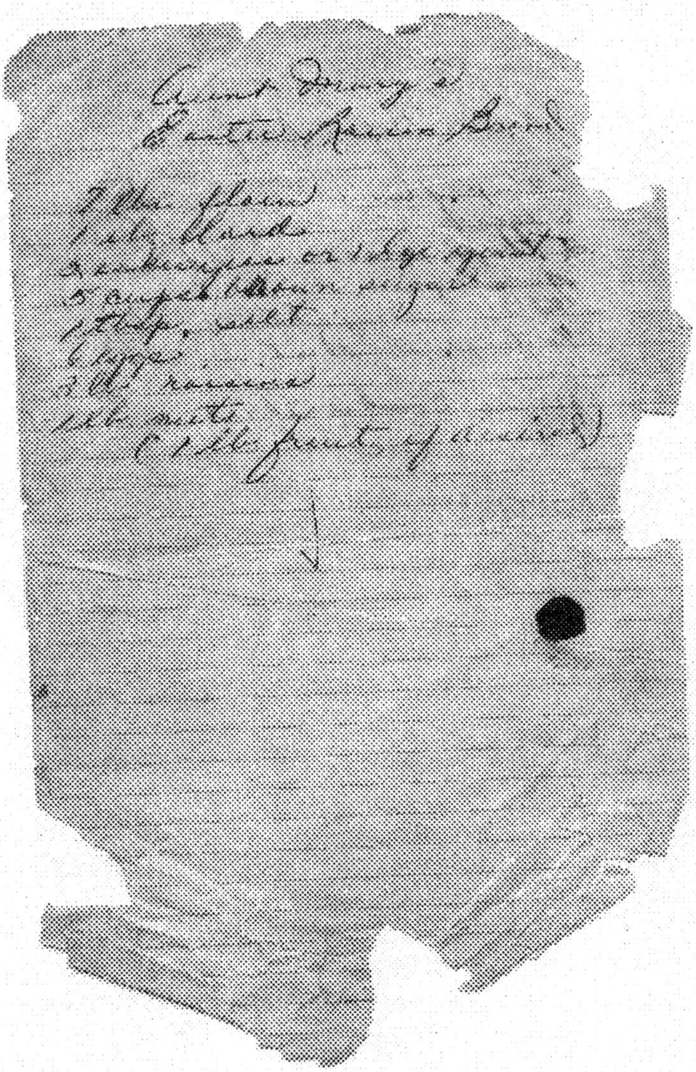

Looking For Something Lost

Looking for something lost
we once a year
join Hank and Harold and Carol
and carol.

It takes us back to little towns
and bedlam becomes Bethlehem again.

Stars shine on little lords
away in mangers

and mothers kneel and watch their children
while shepherds watch their flocks.

We get invited in
for cookies and hot chocolate.

Tears roll down grizzled, smiling faces

and then we leave

just as we left two thousand years ago
crossing the desert
bearing gifts
looking for something lost.

Rose Street Revisited

The Three First Mysteries

She dreamed it was an angel
trying to tell her something.

But it was only someone crying in the garden.
From her window she saw him
plain as night.
The moon fell on his shaking shoulders.
He was alone.
Until the policemen came
and took him away.
She only watched, amazed and frightened.

Back in bed,
she tossed and couldn't sleep.

But she woke up anyway
in the morning
startled by the sudden sun
searing through her window.

At breakfast
no one said a thing about last night,
so she guessed she dreamed it,
the part about the angel
and the part about the man.

She treasured these things in her heart.

Dream or real
Nothing would ever be the same again.

Toots and the Attic Ghost

The reason Dee and I knew there was someone in the attic was that our big brother Toots wrapped on the door every night when he went by.

The long dark hallway started at the bathroom then made a right before the bedrooms on either side and straight ahead. Right there was the attic door. Toots would come home late at night, long after Dee and I and everyone else were in bed, long after we had dozed off. But we'd hear him every night stepping down the black hallway as quietly as he could. At the turn he'd pause. Then he'd wrap: TAP-A-TAP-TAP. Not too loud, but louder than his footsteps. Loud enough to wake us. Then he'd go on to his room across the hall from us. In a few moments we'd be back asleep.

Sometimes one of us said something. "Toots is late tonight" or "It's about time."

Dee was a year older than I was but just as afraid of things she didn't understand. Sometimes to get her going I'd say, "Now it can go back up the stairs to sleep."

"Shut up!" she'd say. The thought of it sitting there waiting on the attic steps scared her. It scared me too, but I said it anyway.

"Don't talk about it. Go back to sleep."

But I'd go on, "It's dragging its bones up the steps now. I think one of 'em fell. Did you hear it clink?"

"Shut up."

"Now it's laying down up there. Hear the boards creak?"

"I'm gonna tell Mama."
"Jeez. Can't I even talk?"
"No. Go back to sleep."
Then I'd turn over and pull the covers with me, listening. I could tell Dee was listening too, because she didn't move.

We knew the attic door was locked and it couldn't get down into the house, but it still scared us being there, sitting on the steps waiting for Toots to get home, or sleeping up there, or doing whatever ghosts do in the daytime or nighttime.

A skeleton key locked it in.

A skeleton key! We had never seen a real ghost, but the ghosts we saw in the movies at the Wilson were usually skeletons. That kind of key would be no problem for any of them. Even dumb people could figure out how to pick a lock that had a skeleton key. Ghosts had to be smarter than dumb people. I'd have to tell Papa about it in the morning so he could put a different kind of lock on it.

But what about tonight? What if it figured out that it might be locked up there with a *skeleton* key and it came back down to try it?

"Dolores," I said. No answer. Did she fall back to sleep already or did she just not want to talk?

Toots was moving around in his bedroom, getting ready for bed. Or was that movement coming from the attic? I listened. The floor creaked, but it had to be the floor in Toots's room. I sat up to make sure. It creaked again.

"Dolores," I said. "Wake up." I shook her.
"What?"

"It's creaking up there."
"I'm gonna tell Mama on you."
"I'm not kidding. Listen."
There was nothing.
"I'm gonna tell Mama." Now she turned away and pulled the covers with her. I yanked them back and lay down.

In the movies at the Wilson ghosts came out at night. It was always in some big house up on a hill where people slept in these huge beds in big rooms with bookcases and fireplaces and candles all over the place. And it was always storming outside. And the wind would blow the windows open and put the candles out. Then the bookcase would swing open real slow and creaky-like, but not loud enough for the girl in the bed who was the main movie star to wake up. And this ugly ghost would creep in.

The scariest one we had ever seen was this one called the Smiling Ghost. He wasn't smiling because he was happy but because his face was just a skull with big teeth and no skin or lips or anything, so it looked like it was smiling. And it wore this black hat for some reason and a kind of cape. I guess it looked like Zorro only it was a ghost. Dee and I and our cousin Georgie ducked under the seats when it came out. Our other cousins, Angelo and Sonny, laughed at us and made fun of us but we stayed down there till the kids stopped screaming and hollering. The ghost always killed everybody but the main guy and the girl. Aunt Lena wouldn't come with us when it was a scary picture, but on Saturday afternoon we could go without her.

31

I was glad there were no bookcases or fireplaces in our bedroom. And no secret passages. I had checked it out long ago. There was just the door and the window. I could take my chances on the window because ghosts never came in from the outside as far as I knew. They were always inside already and sneaking around in secret places at night.

But I kept my eye on the door. I could make out the outline of the door where it was open a couple inches. There was a little bit of moonlight that shined in from the edge of the window blind. Thank God it wasn't storming or raining outside.

Toots had to be kneeling by his bed saying his prayers by now. Sometimes he fell asleep right there before he even got up into bed. I just lay there listening. I only heard Dee breathing in her sleep.

Why did they call it a skeleton key? It was made out of metal not bones. It wasn't shaped like a skeleton. Maybe skeletons made them. Maybe there was this big factory where skeleton ghosts were kept. Like a jail. And all they did was make keys. So we called them skeleton keys.

And our ghost up in the attic had escaped from the Skeleton-Key-Factory-and-Jail and was hiding up there. They sent him one day to deliver keys made in the jail-factory and when he got to our house to deliver the key that we used on the attic door he decided he liked the place, so he was hiding-out here in our attic.

And maybe Toots knew his secret and that's why every night when Toots came home he wrapped on the attic door to let the skeleton know everything was okay and it could go back up the stairs and get some rest.

If that was true, it wouldn't hurt us, even if it did know all about skeleton keys and could pick the lock and come down if it wanted to. It wouldn't want to escape from the attic because that was where it had escaped *to* when it ran away from the Skeleton-Key-Factory-and-Jail.

I wasn't so scared anymore, but I still couldn't sleep. I thought about testing my story on Dee. But she'd be mad if I woke her again.

After awhile, without even thinking twice about it, I slipped out of bed and went to the door. It was pitch black out there in the hallway. I poked my head out and looked down toward the attic door but I couldn't see an inch in front of me.

Then I tried to focus straight across the hall where Toots's room was. I couldn't see it but I held out my hand and let it guide me to his doorknob. It was right there where I reached. I pushed his door open and felt my way across the floor to his bed. I was careful not to trip over him in case he had fallen asleep kneeling there saying his prayers.

"Toots. You awake?"

I heard him move in his bed. "What's a matter?"

"I was thinking about what's in the attic and I couldn't fall back to sleep."

"Nothing's in the attic. Just a bunch of old clothes and junk and stuff."

"Why do you knock then?"

"How many times I have to tell you? I don't know. It's just something I do."

"What makes you do it if you don't know why?"

"I don't know. It's just a habit."

"Something makes you do it. There's something there behind the door waiting for you that makes you—"

"Junior. Go back to bed. You're being crazy now."

"What if it opens the door and comes out?"

"Come on. That's enough of that. Go back to bed."

"It could pick the lock. It's just a skeleton key."

"Look. If you're scared get in bed here with me."

"I'm not scared. I'm just worried."

"Worried or scared. I gotta get some sleep and you do too."

I thought about crawling in bed with Toots, but then I thought about Dee alone across the hall thinking I was there with her. After a moment I felt my way back to Toots's door and then across the black hall into my room. A sliver of moon fell across the bed, just enough to let me see the covers thrown back. And no Dolores.

I screamed and ran out and down to the attic door. I forgot it was locked and pulled on it. I banged on the door, crying, "Bring her back! Bring her back!"

Somebody grabbed me. It was Toots. Bedroom lights were on and Mama was there and Papa and Aunt Lena and Dolly and Rita and Aunt Jessie. I guess I was crying pretty bad and Toots held me and everyone was standing there in their pajamas.

Then down the hall the toilet flushed, the bathroom door opened, and in the light there stood Dee.

"What happened?" she asked.

He Was Only Three

He was only three.
But as he watched the bullies on TV
Surround the child with the red balloon
To snatch it from him and pop it
He cried out, "Let it go! Let it go!"
How could he see, so young,
That letting go was the only way?

Our Own Personal Crow

I can no longer tell whether this comes partly from my memory or entirely from what the family has told me about Christina. It was the late thirties and I was too young then to be sure now. But each Christmas when we watch It's a Wonderful Life, *Uncle Billy's pet crow brings back these "memories" of Christina, our family's own personal crow on Rose Street.*

Uncle Nick Donofrio, Aunt Mary's brother, had never married and so he lived with the DeMarias. He was tall and very thin, with a big wave of white hair that he called a pompadour. He was usually drunk and always funny. Being the second Uncle Nick in the house, he took that name, while Aunt Mary's husband Nick settled for "Zizi Schmack." The "Zizi" was Italian for "uncle." I had no idea what "Schmack" meant until I was much older. Nick DeMaria had been a shoemaker before he came to Youngstown and married Aunt Mary. "Schmack" was just the way ""shoemaker" came out when my Italian elders spoke English.

Anyway, Uncle Nick, the other one, found Christina on a hunting trip. The baby crow had a bad wing and couldn't fly. Uncle Nick felt sorry for her and brought her home

Aunt Mary wasn't happy when her brother staggered up the Rose Street driveway holding the shiny black crow in a crumpled newspaper. But the DeMaria kids and their Leone cousins "oohed" and "ahhed" and cried and giggled and hugged and kissed Uncle Nick, so that Aunt Mary didn't stand a chance. After a while of enjoying all the attention with his new gift, Uncle Nick, as he always did, shrugged his shoulders, muttered something unintelligible, even to those who understood Italian, and went to his room where he kept his bottle. The kids passed the crow around inspecting the anatomy, but there was no clue to its gender, which had to be determined before they named it. The DeMaria and the Leone girls far outnumbered the two boys, my cousin Carmen and my brother Toots, so they agreed that any bird with such shiny black feathers must be a girl. They named her Christina. Once she had a name, that settled all doubts about keeping her.

Christina healed quickly under the tender, loving care of the kids. But, perhaps because of the nature of the injury, she would never fly again. Or maybe she just didn't want to. She came to feel part of the family. When the kids played in the yard we shared with Aunt Mary, she hopped around them, squawking and generally getting in the way and making a nuisance of herself, the way a baby brother or sister would, too young to play but wanting to anyway. When no people were in the yard, she flew up to her perch on the clothesline post and observed or slept or said nasty things to whoever passed through the yard.

You see, Christina was no ordinary crow. She talked. Whole sentences, in English with an Italian accent. Someone told Aunt Mary that if you split the tongue of a crow you can teach it to talk. Aunt Mary refused to let anyone do this to Christina, but the crow talked anyway.

True, she spoke short sentences. Her grammar was that of a five-year-old child. But her vocabulary went beyond that into round, solid Italian oaths. If the tongue had been split, maybe sewing it back could have stopped the swearing. But she swore without a split tongue, so there was nothing to sew up again to stop her.

Up on her clothesline perch, Christina called out names and curses to those neighbors who passed through on their way to Conti's store or to St. Francis Church on Shehy Street.

Several theories circulated about the source of the swear words that colored Christina's speech. Some said it was the neighborhood boys. Others blamed the men, returning drunk from the Ritz Bar.

But Christina wasn't all embarrassment. She had her practical value. Legend has it that Christina squawked out "Grandpa, get up!" every morning when it was time for Beatangelo to rise for work. Christina also announced the various neighbors and family friends. "Compare Pasquale!" she'd call out, and we knew who had entered the yard. And when Aunt Mary's Angela was ready for school, she stood on her porch and called for Clara at the Febo house two doors up from us. "Clara" she called once and Christina took up the call until Clara came running out her side door and across the Carney's back yard to meet Angela for the walk to school.

Aunt Helen, Uncle Freddy's wife, routinely exchanged insults with Christina when she passed the crow's perch on her way to or from her house up on Fruit Street. They stood eye to eye and

exchanged Italian insults. Imagine the scene: Aunt Helen, always dressed to the hilt with not a hair out of place, the very picture of decorum, engaged in a toe to toe verbal battle with a bird.
"Stupida!" Aunt Helen said.
"Stupida!" Christina said back.
The exchange continued until Christina failed to respond. Aunt Helen turned and continued on her way.
"Stupida!" Christina called after her.
Aunt Helen spun and glared. Christina glared back. A standoff.
"Aunt Helen whispered "Stupida" under her breath, turned and walked away.
"Stupida! Stupida! Stupida! Stupida!" came in quick volleys from the bird, fluttering her feathers.
Christina liked to hop around on the bricks around us as we played hopscotch or kick the can in the yard between our house and Aunt Mary's. She wasn't afraid of us, but Dolores and I were young enough to be a little afraid of her.
Yet as time passed and the older kids stopped making a fuss over her and giving her the attention she craved, we younger ones got used to her hopping and squawking beside us while we played. We hardly noticed her. She came to seem commonplace, as if talking crows were a normal part of life in the neighborhood.
Neither we nor Aunt Mary had dogs or cats, and the neighbors were pretty good about keeping their pets out of our yard, so Christina was relatively safe there.

Yet, there's no haven entirely protected from the outside world. Our yard served as a common passageway between Rose Street and Shehy Street. A simple gate separated our back yard from Conti's garden path, which led to their driveway and on to their store at Shehy. All the neighbors and sometimes strangers used this as a shortcut through the neighborhood to the store or to Saint Francis or to visit friends on a neighboring street.

One summer afternoon several kids from Murdock Street—which ran perpendicular to Shehy right across from Conti's—took this shortcut. Their dog trotted along beside them, a dirty white little mongrel that stopped to sniff everything in sight.

Normally Christina managed to hop up to her clothesline perch in an emergency. This time she didn't make it. Squawks and growls and children's screams shattered the calm of this summer day. The whole Leone and DeMaria families and some of the Rose Street neighbors were suddenly out of doors yelling.

The dog bolted back through Conti's yard with its captive flapping in its mouth. The Murdock kids gave loud chase, followed by Leones and DeMarias, Febos and Palumbos, Vagnarellis and Carneys. Dolores, probably four or five years old at the time, and I, maybe three, toddled along in terror beside Aunt Lena, who cried loudly. We ran Through Conti's path, along their driveway to Shehy, and across to Murdock, to mid-block.

Suddenly the chase stopped.

The front runners circled the porch of a house, where the thief had stolen with its catch.

Children pleaded. Grown ups swore in several languages. The villain paid no heed. Finally someone fed one of the smaller Murdock kids through an opening of broken slats. G r o w l i n g and rustling, then silence. Deadly silence. An eternity of seconds.

    The boy's tear streaked face was first to emerge. Then, with a tug from his brother, the rest of him. In the boy's grip lay a lifeless pile of sparkling, bloody feathers.

    The dog stayed behind, in the darkness, silent.

    Bitter words hit the air like the beginning of a storm, got gradually louder, then, just as quickly, subsided. The Murdock kids cried. Their parents apologized profusely and swore and smacked at them. The dog still refused to make an appearance. The crowd slowly dispersed.

    There was a brief debate among the Rose Street kids over who would bear the remains. As it turned out several Rose Street boys divided the honors among them. There were feathers enough to go around. Dolores and I were too sad and of course too squeamish to offer our palms. The funeral procession back to Rose Street was tearful, yet as wordless and solemn as the chase had been frantic.

    After a futile attempt at reconstruction, we gave Christina's feathers a proper burial in a corner of the yard, with a stick cross marking their grave.

    I remember none of these details, but Dolores tells me that she and I reenacted the saga of Christina's last moments with great emotion, playing the various parts tearfully between us for any in the neighborhood who would lend us their ears.

This was my earliest "remembered" encounter with death, certainly with sudden, unnecessary death. A family member had been snatched away by something outside my safe world on Rose Street.

I knew from that time that it could happen.

Pepper Passes

Danny:

But she said Pepper's dead
the brown grass the mud along the ditch said dead
but dead what dead how
another day she said dead it was Aunt Mary
the mud sucks pulls at my shoes she won't like
that
Aunt Mary's dead she said
does that mean I said does that mean she won't
come anymore
with her black sweater
and hold me on her lap and sing those songs
that funny way so I knew what she sang
and laughed at what she sang
but didn't understand the words
yes she said yes
the water runs fast there but doesn't run here on
top
only on the bottom
and the brown grass and brush say dead
Pepper's dead
and Aunt Mary
and the man in the black car they went to see
they saw in the paper
the paper says who's dead
and they get dressed up and go to see
the paper said Aunt Mary
did the paper say Pepper
or did someone else tell them

the brown grass and the mud along the ditch
my shoes my muddy shoes
she won't like that
but won't say so
because Pepper's dead
and she knows I can't help the mud
no more than the water in the ditch can help the mud
that mixes with it
no more than Aunt Mary or Pepper
I'M COMING
I'"M COMING BACK
I JUST CAME OUT TO WATCH THE DITCH

A Sonnet for My Son

That day you offered me a melody
as you and I, my son, sat breakfasting:
You sang on wedding plans and family
and jobs and cars and—almost everything.

But what you really tried to sing, I know
(Yes, I have sung myself that very song),
was something about love, and how we go
away and still remain behind us all along.

But I can't phrase it anymore than you,
and so I harmonized about the plate
(called Grand Slam? All-American?) and who
Would pay and waitresses who made us wait.

Yes, my son, if you got the lyrics wrong
and couldn't phrase it, still I heard your song.

Date 5-6 194_

Mr. & Mrs. C. _____

No. _____

Reg. No.	Clerk	ACCOUNT FORWARDED		
1	Fish			22
2	cake			5
3	cheese			10
4	margarine			10
5	Oats			1
6	apples			10
7	W. [?]			20
8	peas			25
9	crackers			10
10	oranges			16
11	milk			13
12	M & [?]			13
13	[?]			13
14				7 81
15				

Your account stated to date. If error is found return at once.

Rose Street Revisited

Louisa May Alcott

Louisa May Alcott
...and then again she may not.

The Wilson

Drive by the site today, the building still stands, even the side attachment that was the Sweet Shoppe. But it's so much smaller than he remembers it. And it's sadly unkempt, weeds and tree branches sprout half way up its sides and droop their ragged arms haphazardly.

There's no sign that it was once a movie theater, no marquee, no box office at the front. Just a shell of the structure it once was. The life of the magical picture shows oozed out long ago and the body decays in the sight of all who pass by.

He entered the world when the worst of the Depression was over. The War had not yet come. Neither had television. They were poor, but he didn't know that. So was everyone else in his real world of Rose Street. They had shoes and other clothing and there was always food. Really good food. As for mental and spiritual nourishment, there was plenty of that too.

But there was also the world of the rich and famous, who danced and sang and emoted before him only on the silver screen at the Wilson along with the cowboys and pirates and superheroes. There wasn't much there that he could relate to his own life. Maybe the Dead End Kids, Our Gang, and Fat and Skinny frolicked in surroundings he recognized, but he saw early on that life was never really like that. As for Fred and Ginger, Tracy and Hepburn, Bogey and Bacall, they met, lost, and found each other again someplace very far East, West, North, and South of Rose Street in Youngstown, Ohio. They might as well have resided on some star that was barely visible in his red, smoky, night sky.

But he loved the world Hollywood fed him and his family several times a week at the Wilson. The theater was small and plain, with two sections of not very comfortable seats accessible from a center aisle or, narrowly, a side aisle whose approach was almost blocked by a concession stand that lured them with its buttered popcorn smell each time they passed. The rest rooms were in the basement, dark, not very clean, smelling a bit of urine. It was scary going down there, so sometimes Aunt Lena had to go with them. They tried to use the bathroom at home just before they left, but usually they had to make the descent at least one time.

Sometimes, when a really big picture was playing downtown, Aunt Lena or one of the other grownups took him and his sister Dolores and maybe his cousin Sonny or Georgie to the Warner or the Palace or the Paramount and he watched the picture show in luxurious surroundings that matched the homes of the stars.

But the Wilson was more comfortable. The double features changed three times a week in there and they religiously attended.

That is, they attended if the "Legion of Decency" movie ratings in each Friday's Catholic Exponent found the films morally unobjectionable. "Low moral tone" was a frequent offense. More specific evils: "suicide in plot solution," murder in plot solution," "divorce in plot solution," and "condones adultery." The kids weren't sure what that last one meant but they were pretty sure they wouldn't be committing any of those other sins any time soon. On the screen blood was rare and girls' breasts and other normally covered body parts were never bared. Except through implication that the kids never picked up on, sex was absent. Physical contact was limited to hugs and brief pecks on the face. Rhett Butler was the only one allowed to say "Damn," and he shocked the world when he said it.

They walked, excited with anticipation, the three blocks down to the Wilson in the evenings, and they walked home in the dark, still excited over the glamorous world they had witnessed in the dark anonymity of the small theater. On Saturdays they were sometimes allowed to go without an adult, though Aunt Lena, child that she was, usually accompanied them. They'd sit laughing and squealing, cheering and groaning through features and cartoons and newsreels and serials, munching on popcorn and Milk Duds or struggling with Black Cows.

He remembered the many times he and Dolores and Georgie had to duck under the seats when things got too scary, as in The Smiling Ghost. They actually ran out of the theater when the terror struck in The Uninvited. Angelo and Sonny stayed, but they were older and could take it.

He remembered the Saturday afternoon serials, Don Winslow of the Navy, Batman, Gangbusters. They had to wait a whole week to see how the hero got out of the jam he was in at the end of each installment.

He remembered "Bank Night," which was always on a weeknight because it was for the grownups, but he felt the excitement anyway of Aunt Lena possibly winning a beautiful set of dishes.

The day he remembered most was a September afternoon when Uncle John, the manager, stopped the movie and ran to the stage to announce the Japanese surrender. World War II was finally over. Cheers went up and continued as the theater emptied. They ran home with Aunt Lena crying for them to wait for her. They found that the whole neighborhood was at Saint Francis church offering thanks to God.

The Wilson was as important a part of his young life as was this church, where he was an altar boy and fancied himself a devout Christian. St. Francis of Assisi fed his soul. The worldly Wilson Theater fed his imagination.

Rose Street Revisited

Christopher, David, and Danny, and Gene

Christopher, David, and Danny, and Gene
went for a ride in their homemade machine,
traveled from here all the way to the moon,
didn't return till the middle of June,
laughed when their Mommy looked down in surprise
with a where-have-you-been kind of look in her eyes.
"We've been to the moon and we've seen what we've
      seen,"
said Christopher, David, and Danny, and Gene.

It was almost a year they were gone to the moon,
but with magic it happened from breakfast till noon,
while Mom washed the dishes and scrubbed up the floor
and wiped off the prints from the dining room door.

"And what did you see when you went on your trip
all the way to the moon on your kitchen chair ship?"

Christopher, David, an Danny, and Gene

Now each one had thoughts of what he might
have seen,
but he couldn't quite say them in words, except
Gene,
who said "gaga" and "google" and "gorgle" and
"glay,"
so those couldn't count as real words anyway.

All the others could say was they went there
    somehow,
and they saw lots of things, and were gone until
now.

No one has discovered the things that were seen
by Christopher, David, and Danny, and Gene.

State Zitto e Mangiate

As a first generation Italian-American (both my parents were born in Italy), I've tried to preserve the traditions that I grew up with in raising my own family. In a world like ours, this is bound to be an uphill battle. I'm forever grateful that my children, all now grown and on their own, love the traditions, especially (of course) those involving food. My mother, Josephine, was a great cook, and we were fortunate enough to have her with us and active while her grandkids were growing. In their older years my parents shared a home with my brother Ray's family. His six children were especially blessed with her daily meals.

All the grandchildren have great memories of Mom's cooking. She presided over holidays and other family celebrations. Besides the delicious food itself, there was her presence, loving, yes, but also assertive. She was in command and we all knew it. Whenever the chatter started to interfere with the eating, she said, "*State zitto e mangiate,*" which came out in her Abruzzese dialect as *stattazeet a mange*—Shut up and eat!

We were all delighted back in the spring of 1995, thirteen years after my mother's death, when my nephew Joe (one of Ray's sons) and two of my boys, Gene and Chris, decided to open their own restaurant, which Joe named—you guessed it— "State Zitto e Mangiate."

First you should understand that when I say "their own restaurant," I mean that loosely. They

State Zitto e Mangiate

had no physical building they could call theirs. They had no capital to buy one. They had simply the concept. Yet Joe was the baker at the off-campus coffeehouse called The Beat, near Youngstown State University. He convinced the owners to rent him the place on Saturday nights, when it was closed for business anyway, since its clientele was largely the breakfast and lunch crowd on school days.

A former mansion, the coffee house had a small but adequate kitchen and four small dining areas, two downstairs and two up, enough to seat thirty-five people at most. The boys figured that with the limited space and kitchen facilities, they could handle twice that number in an evening if they carefully scheduled different seating times. In true Italian tradition, they weren't much concerned about long waits between courses. While the kitchen might be a madhouse of preparation, the dining areas were for leisurely eating with good conversation and companionship in between.

The meals in 1995 would cost each patron a flat $11.00 for the basic pasta or $13.00 for the fancy. The helpers would share the tips. Once the bills were paid there would be no money to count as profit.

But the boys didn't do this for the money. They knew it would be hard, tiring work, but they'd love it. It would be their grandmother come back to spend an evening with them. It was their roots. It was their love for each other that they knew they expressed best when they worked hard together on something that linked them to their past.

Joe set down two firm rules:

No meat would be used. Joe, a vegetarian, maintained that in the poor villages in the Abruzzi, where our people were from, they didn't eat much meat anyway. The truth is that none of us were about to debate the matter with him, because, whether or not we were meat-eaters ourselves, we were all aware of his ability to create delicious meatless dinners.

Each dish would be homemade and prepared from scratch. Early in the week, Joe decided on the menu. Then he shopped. On Thursdays, the boys gathered with any family volunteers at Joe's parents' house to make the pasta. The finished basement had the facilities and large enough tables where the pasta could be laid out as it was made. In the upstairs kitchen the sauce bubbled, while vegetables and fruits, salads, and desserts were cut and prepared, filling the home with the aromas of Italy. Joe baked the bread in the coffee house ovens the afternoon of each dinner.

In the meantime, reservations were taken by phone at the coffeehouse. Normally within a day the list was full.

The evening of the dinner, the workers, both family and friends, manned the kitchen and the dining areas, converting the college coffee house to give it an Italian flavor: place mats of red and green, Italian music on the stereo, flowers on the tables, candles on the windowsills and tables, whatever could be used for atmosphere. I usually arrived early to help set up.

Besides Joe, Gene, and Chris, as many young family and friends jammed the kitchen as were able to help with the cooking, slicing, stirring, washing, and the required singing and shouting. Sometimes I worked in the kitchen too, mainly trying not to be in the way. They'd have done as well without me, but it made me young again to stir the bubbling sauce or slice the pungent garlic clove, taking orders, along with the younger crew, from my nephew and sons.

As guests arrived, my daughter Gina usually acted as hostess and cashier. Another daughter, Teresa, and her boyfriend Tony waited tables, along with whoever else among friends and family volunteered. Tony's ethnic background is Polish. He is blonde and a man of few words, not the Italian waiter type. Yet, in an apron he became *il cameriere perfetto*. "My name is Antonio," he'd say, "and I will be your waiter." He took orders and served, and inquired after his diners' needs with the best of them.

My son Dan, visiting from San Francisco, took a couple turns at waiting tables. Dan's a restaurant critic who has had a lifelong love affair with food, especially meat dishes, so here he was both in and out of his element. The unofficial family clown, Dan chewed on a crust of warm bread dipped in sauce as he waited tables, and sometimes helped himself to leftovers on plates as he carried them away. No one minded. He was being Dan.

One of the regulars among the irregulars

waiting tables was Joe's brother Raym, a doctor by profession, who would dash over after his calls, doff his necktie, don his Italian apron, and commence taking orders.

In fact, the average education of the servers was beyond the Master's degree. Except for the family members, waiters and other help, close friends of the family, were as likely not to be of Italian background as to be. For the night they were *paesanos*.

Guests brought their own wine—usually home made. They could purchase tea, soft drinks, and coffee, in all the varieties one should expect of a coffee shop. Each table had a bowl of Italian olives, artichoke hearts, *lupini*, and a basket of the most delicious, crusty bread, hot from the oven.

The menu typically began with a *prima piatta* offering two choices each evening of fried greens, *polenta*, eggplant parmesan, roasted red peppers, sautéed mushrooms, steamed beans or broccoli or artichokes, or a soup: wedding, or something uncommon like mushroom or basil potato or artichoke.

The *secondi piatti* or main course consisted of a choice of two pasta dishes: something fancy like manicotti, ravioli, or la sagna; or plain old spaghetti, linguini, or fettuccini. Joe gave a choice of traditional tomato sauce (but, of course, meatless) or something exotic, like basil cream or dried tomato or red pepper cream sauce. No one could be disappointed by either. (See a sample menu)

The *contorni*, the salad, came in two choices: a garden salad (with endive and Roman lettuce, sometimes dandelion, purple cabbage, carrots, black olives, red peppers, and pepperoncini), and a specialty salad, such as an endive walnut, a cucumber, or the *Louisa Salada*, one of Joe's Mom's specialties, a mixture of celery, black olives, cheese, oil, and vinegar.

Desserts were either fresh fruit or something special, like biscotti or a lemon or linzer torte or one or two choices of my daughter Andi's pies, such as nectarine, butter rum pecan, apple, or mixed berry.

For each course, quantity was to the boys as important as quality. Servings were heaped on the plate. If a diner did empty a plate the waiter was quick to offer more. Refusals triggered phrases familiar to my childhood: What'sa matter? You sick? You eat like a bird. No one went away hungry.

The pacing was leisurely, as it should be when dining is a social experience. Guests came in twos or in larger groups, sometimes ten or twelve to a group, and made an evening of it, with Italian music of all styles, Pavarotti to Dino, providing the background for talk and laughter and moans and sighs and all the funny noises that signal satisfaction.

After the guests had dined and gone on their happy way, the workers cleaned, sat to dinner themselves, and cleaned again. It was well after midnight when they locked up and went home.

After a couple months, the every week experience became too much to make it fun anymore, so the boys cut back to every other week. Even so, the demand on Joe's time took its toll. When eventually Chris's work called him out of town and Gene made plans to go out to San

Francisco to visit his brother, it was an easy decision to suspend the restaurant operation.

After several months off, when all three boys were finally back in town, they planned a one-nighter: New Year's Eve of 1995. They packed them in, but the awareness that Gene and Chris were both leaving the state after the holiday put a damper on the feast. State Zitto would become a memory.

During the next couple years, whenever all three were in town at the same time—a rarity— talk of a stata zitto weekend would surface. Several times the talk became a reality, but only for a weekend or two.

Today, Joe lives in California, Gene lives—well, wherever he happens to be—and Chris has his own construction business here in Youngstown that keeps him busy. The chances of resurrecting the restaurant are dim.

This past Christmas it just happened that all three were home for the family Christmas party that we now hold between the holidays. The various family groups brought casseroles and desserts, but the boys occupied the kitchen. Under Joe's supervision they made the pizza. The dough was from scratch. The delicious smell of the pizza sauce permeated the warm kitchen air. The pizza was served with and without tomato sauce. It was topped with olives, or peppers, or mushrooms, but, of course, no meat. Helping the boys in the kitchen and observing the others pitching in, listening to the boys bantering back and forth, I was transported back to the restaurant experience.

Now, whenever I reflect on the passing of the wonderful people and times of my youth, more recent memories of the Christmas pizza party blend with *State Zitto Mangiate*. Once again I dine with my friends and survey the room of happy eaters and happy workers. The gap between then and now fades, and my mother emerges from the kitchen. All hungry eyes turn towards her—those of my generation and of my children and even their *children*.

Her eyes sparkle with the joy of the feast. She says, *Stattazeet a mange*!

On the menu at the last dinner, held on March 28, 1998, Joe puts the experience into his own words:

State Zitto e Mangiate

"State Zitto e Mangiate," which you should pronounce statazeet a mange and which means "shut up and eat," is sort of a phantom restaurant. It used to exist here at the Beat Coffeehouse on certain Friday or Saturday evenings. Then it didn't. Then it did. Then it didn't exist anywhere for a long time, except—I like to think—in the hearts of our most faithful customers.

For me "Statazeet" is a little like a friend from out of town who comes for a long visit. When he's gone you notice how quiet and empty the house is, but for the most part you're still glad he's gone. My cousins/partners Chris and Gene have always had a better attitude about these dinners than I have, but it's not like I'd let them do it without me.

...

If you're a new customer, what you need to know is that I'm not a businessman, obviously, or even a very serious cook. About all I am is stubborn. What I'm stubborn about is requiring that everything we serve, from the bread to the macaroni to the sauces to the dessert, be made from scratch and to the best of our ability. I do things the way I like to do them, hoping you'll like them that way too. If you don't, to be honest, I'd rather not know—unless it's something having to do with Chris.

Now as I've said before: Be patient. Be nice. Be sure your dinner companion is someone you like to spend time with. And don't make funny noises at the dinner table.

- Joe Leone

Dom

> "Life a funny thing."
> —Sonny Liston

In the cabin in Vermont
Dom tacked this on his wall.

Without the verb it's funny.
With it it's just as true.
Dom knew that.
Twisted ankles,
falling off cliffs,
divorces.
Full of life, he made us laugh
("Oops! Sorry. Wrong chord.")

Dying, he confused us,
but only now and then.
Every other now and then we laughed still
and still laugh.

Once there was a child
who grew up
to tell us to become children again.

Dom listened.

To Andi

Take with you, Andi, as you travel down
into the harried world where grownups live,
as much of childhood as your soul can bear:
take wonder and delight and joy of life;
take unencumbered love and innocence.
That when the sorrows start to overwhelm
these simple things may buoy you up and out,
back to the child that you have always been,
into the kingdom that our Lord described,
that Heaven of a higher innocence.
May you, my daughter, journeying through life,
always a lady, always be a child.

Guitar Blues

Junior was really happy when Sonny came to live with them. Uncle Dom asked Mama if Sonny could stay on Rose Street for a while till he got his affairs settled. Sonny was eleven months older, but that gave Junior a buffer between himself and Uncle Fred's Angelo (Sonny was an Angelo too) and his sister Dolores. They were both almost two years older than Junior, and so when they all played together they looked at Junior as just a kid, like they looked at his other cousin Georgie. She *was* just a kid, almost two years younger than Junior. With Sonny around he would have someone closer to his own age, a buddy to team up with him instead of Angelo and Dee.

That was his thinking. The truth was Sonny was closer to their age than to his, so now there would be a third one to team up against him and Georgie.

But it really wasn't too bad. Sonny would live in his house. Even sleep in the same bed with him. And, through the quirks of school registration, they were in the same grade in school. These things would give him the edge.

There were just a couple other problems. Uncle Dom was a Yankee fan, so Sonny rooted for them too.

"How can you be Italian and not root for the Yankees?" Uncle Dom asked, even though the Yankees were way far away in some other state and Cleveland was right here in Northeastern Ohio with them. "Look who they got. They got DiMaggio, for Christ's sake. They got Rizzuto, Frankie Crosetti. They got this new catcher Berra comin' up. You don't see no Italians playing for Cleveland. You never will."

But how could anyone root for a team, DiMaggio or not, that won all the time? There was nothing to hope for, nothing to worry about. It didn't make sense. The Yankees were almost away in some other country and Cleveland was right here in their own back yard. It was like rooting for Germany!

But Uncle Dom was a Yankee fan so Sonny was too.

Another problem was Sonny wasn't too interested in school. He put about two seconds into his homework after school and went running out to play with Angelo and the other Rose Street kids. And Mama wouldn't yell at Sonny the way she did at him or Dee if they didn't do their homework. It made Junior look bad. Junior took school seriously and got all A's, which kind of made him look bad in the neighborhood anyway. He had to get his homework just right, so Sonny was out there with Angelo and the neighbor kids playing ball, while he was still doing his homework, getting it perfect. It gave him a bad name.

And Sonny was a good athlete, which made Junior look all the worse. Sonny ran faster and hit, threw, and caught the ball better. This helped when they played on the same side, but Sonny usually managed to get on Angelo's side and they only picked Junior and the girls, Dee and Georgie, if they had to. Sometimes they even picked Dee before him.

But the Yankees were a problem only in the summer, and the school thing and ballgame thing were there even before Sonny came to live with them. The truth is the positive things about having Sonny around far outweighed the negative.

They became brothers. They served Mass together over at Saint Francis and got to pal around with Father Sofranec and Genie Kaulis and Victor Markasky, the older altar boys. They went to the movies together. They walked downtown together and ate lunch at Stone's Grill where Sonny's mother, Aunt Frances, worked and always treated them like grown-up businessmen when she waited on them, but always paid the bill herself. Sometimes when the Yankees were in town Mama even let them catch the train to Cleveland to see a Sunday doubleheader. The war was over and DiMaggio was back, but so was Bob Feller back pitching for the Indians. Junior and Sonny each learned to show respect for the other's feelings, but sometimes the train ride back home was a really long one, even if the teams split.

And he got to hang out a lot with Uncle Dom now that Sonny was around. They went fishing sometimes to Milton Dam. The fishing was fun itself but they also got to stop at the Wave and have a hamburger and a 7-Up. And Uncle Dom took the two of them with him when he went to Mugsy's bar to drop off the bug slips. Sometimes they not only got a 7-Up but they got to shoot pool while they waited for Uncle Dom to take care of his business. Junior stunk at it, but he could feel himself getting the hang of it, and once he even came close to beating Sonny.

One of the best things was they got to go with Uncle Dom to parties and things to hear Queenie Miller play his guitar. Queenie Miller was the best guitar player in the world. Ask Uncle Dom. He used to play in some big band like Benny Goodman or someone like that, and he was just too good to stay there, so he came back to Youngstown to pal around with Uncle Dom and his friends Mugsy and Bat Eye and Smash and play some music whenever they got together.

He loved the times when Queenie Miller played those sweet songs and Uncle Dom sang in his tenor voice, especially those Ink Spot and Mills Brothers songs. He wished he could sing but most of all he prayed he could learn to play like that.

Then something happened. Summer was over and the Yankees were finished winning the World Series, so Uncle Dom talked to Mama about the boys taking guitar lessons. It would cost $1.25 a half-hour downtown at the Strouss' Music Center. They could pay $2.50 for an hour and take their lessons together.

Mama was reluctant. That was a lot of money to dish out every week. But Uncle Dom convinced her that the only way Sonny would practice would be if Junior took lessons with him. Junior's good study habits would brush off on Sonny and make him want to keep up.

Mama was a sucker for anything Uncle Dom wanted, so she agreed.

Junior was excited. He would learn to play like Queenie Miller!

Sonny was not excited. He wanted to play

Guitar Blues

the trumpet, not the guitar.
"What are you crazy?" his father said. "All these people living in this house and you want to play the trumpet? Grandpa and Aunt Jo and Uncle Carmen and this whole neighborhood would have a fit with all the racket. Mary the Green House and Mrs. Palumbo and Delia and the whole East Side'd be wantin' to kill me. Besides, the guitar is nice and quiet and you can sing along with it. How you gonna sing along with a trumpet when your lips are all tied up and your blastin' everyone's eardrums?"

So Uncle Dom bought Sonny this nice used Gretsch and he got Junior this little folk guitar and he took them downtown for their first lesson with Mr. Johnny Mraz at the Strouss' Music Center.

Sonny grumbled all the way, but Junior was excited. He would take his lessons as seriously as his schoolwork and practice twice as much as he needed, and before long he'd have a crowd gathered around him wherever they went. Him and Queenie Miller would be playing sweet music together and maybe even the Mills Brothers would ask him to join them some day, and he could tour the whole country strumming and picking out "Lazy River" and "Someday" and numbers like that, and all the neighbors on Rose Street would go downtown to the Palace or over to the Club Merry-Go-Round or out to the Idora Park Ballroom to hear him when the Mills Brothers came to town.

He would even try to help Sonny learn, poor kid, maybe give him some encouragement, so he could strum along when they played with Queenie Miller or the Mills Brothers or Benny Goodman.

Rose Street Revisited

Then, in the first lesson something happened that shook his whole faith in the idea of justice in the universe.

No matter what Mr. Mraz asked him to do, he struggled. He was all thumbs. His guitar buzzed and burped and bleated, but it wouldn't sing.

Sonny, on the other hand, put his guitar in position on his lap, listened to Mr. Mraz and—presto—began to strum what actually sounded like music. Yes, it was music. He watched Mr. Mraz switch from the C chord to the C7th and he did it. To the F—an impossible feat for a beginner—and it sounded like an F chord. Pure. No buzz. Junior tried it and it sounded like a cow dying in the backyard.

Beginner's luck? If only that were so.

The experience made Junior practice more than he had intended. He practiced till his fingertips almost bled. Each evening after school he rushed through his homework, grabbed his guitar, and soured up the bedroom with the most atrocious noises. As evenings passed it got worse. Dolores from her room across the hall yelled for him to play quieter so she could concentrate on her schoolwork. Rita and Dolly and Toots tried to stifle laughter.

At the supper table Dolores complained to Mama to make him stop the racket.

"He thinks if he bangs on it louder it'll sound better," she said, "but then we all have to suffer."

"*Statta zeeta mangia!*" Mama said.

"Well, how come when Sonny practices we can't hear him?" Dolores asked.

Sonny shot a glance at Junior.

Guitar Blues

'Cause he doesn't practice, Junior thought. He didn't say it aloud. If they made Sonny actually practice, he'd really that could be worse for Junior.

Papa smiled. Sonny went back to eating, eager to finish and get back outside to play.

Only Aunt Lena tried to be nice about it. "I can't wait till you learn to play something," she said, peaking in his bedroom while he practiced. "Or *are* you playing something?"

After several days of exasperation, Junior even allowed himself to commit a sin he'd have to tell Father Sofranec about on Saturday at Confession. He allowed himself to think, "Sure, he gets that nice Gretsch and I get this cheap old guitar. It's made all backwards and I bet even Queenie Miller couldn't make it sound good."

On the evening of the same day this wicked thought jeopardized his soul, when Sonny was out playing, Junior shut the door to their bedroom and took Sonny's guitar out of its case. He examined it. It was bigger, really too big for him. Its neck was even narrower, so the strings were closer together, which made it harder to press the right strings. Even worse, the bridge was so high that the strings were raised. When he pressed as hard as he could, they still buzzed. The sound was even worse than when he played his own guitar. How could Sonny get those smooth sounds out of this?

Junior's one consolation, as that first week passed, was that Sonny didn't practice at all. It was as if he didn't even know he had a lesson to learn. When Uncle Dom stopped in and asked how they were doing with the "box," as he called the guitar,

77

Junior said an unenthusiastic "Okay."

Sonny flipped a softball back and forth from his bare hand to his gloved hand, anxious to get outside and play. "Good," he said.

"Let's hear something. You know any songs yet?" he asked Sonny.

"Polly Wolly Doodle," I threw in. "It's only two chords."

"It's a sissy song," Sonny said.

"What are you talkin' about?" Uncle Dom said. "I know that song. "That's a good song."

"It only has two chords," Junior said with authority. "That's why we're learning that first."

"You can't be impatient," Uncle Dom said, still talking to Sonny. "You'll learn some better songs as you go along."

'We're learning 'Old Black Joe" next week," Junior said. "It has an F chord."

Sonny threw the softball a little higher.

"Put that damn ball down for a minute, will y'?" Uncle Dom said. "You gotta take this guitar stuff serious. You payin' attention to me when I talk?"

Sonny stuffed the ball in his glove. "Sure, Dad. It's just that we got a game goin' out there. They're waitin' for me."

"You gotta practice every night if you wanna play some songs you like."

"I know, Dad."

"Practice like Junior here. You guys oughtta practice together."

"Sure, Dad."

"That F chord's a tough one," Junior said,

shaking his head.

    The evening of the second lesson arrived, and, try as he might, Junior's strumming was still awful. His finger tips ached, but he was determined to practice right up until the time Uncle Dom picked them up to take them downtown.

    Except for Junior's little inspection, Sonny's guitar hadn't been out of the case for a week and Junior felt bad for him. But it was his own fault. Uncle Dom would yell at him when he found out he wasn't practicing. Junior had reminded him in the morning, at school, and on the way home from school, but Sonny still hadn't taken out his guitar.

    Then a half-hour before time to leave, Sonny came busting into the bedroom, sweaty from playing ball. He grabbed his Gretch from the case, opened his lesson book, and stared at it. Junior, in sympathy, put his guitar in its cardboard case and carried it from the room. He tiptoed downstairs, grabbed his jacket, and waited at the kitchen table for their ride.

    In the studio, Sonny went first. He strummed through the chords of "Polly Wolly Doodle" flawlessly as Mr. Mraz tapped his knee beside him. He even got fancy, halfway through and jazzed up the beat. Mr. Mraz scolded him, even as he shook his head in delight, and had him slip back to the basic 1-2-3-4 strum.

    Then it was Junior's turn. The C chord sounded almost clear as he strummed it eight times while he sang in his head, "Oh I went—down South for to—see my Sal—sing Polly Wolly Doodle—all the..." Then it seemed like several days elapsed while he tried to move that index finger down one string at the same time he moved the middle and third fingers up one for the G7th chord and sang in his mind the word "day." He tried to make up for the lapse by swishing through the next eight beats in double time: "MySalsheamaspunkygalsingPollyWollyDoodleallthe" Then another long struggle back to a C chord and—"day." The buzzing made the three of them shudder.

 Mr. Mraz turned away and pulled at his tie. Sonny flipped furiously through the pages of his lesson book. Mr. Mraz turned back, took the guitar from Junior's lap gingerly, as if it had some disease, and held it at arm's length, turning it to inspect it from every angle, as a carpenter would inspect a board. He handed the guitar back. "Try it again," Mr. Mraz said, clearing his throat, "from the top."

 In that hour somebody kept going down South for to see this Sal girl many times over. Spunky gal that she was, Sal would have run farther and farther South, all the way to the Gulf, just to avoid contact with *that* troubadour.

 It was a long ride home, and a longer week, and longer and longer weeks after that. Junior practiced so hard that he neglected his schoolwork. The weekly confrontations with Mr. Mraz were pure agony for him. Sonny silently witnessed every second of humiliation without even cracking a smile so Junior could hold it against him.

 Sonny didn't practice at all except for the few minutes just before Uncle Dom arrived each lesson night for the trip downtown. Yet he effortlessly picked and strummed his way through whatever songs were set before him!

Whenever Queenie Miller showed up for a family party and they gathered to listen and sing along, Sonny strummed along with him. Junior took his place somewhere in the crowd with Dee, Angelo, and Georgie.

One evening, after many months had passed; Uncle Dom called Junior aside.

"I want to tell you thanks, Junior, for keeping Sonny going with the guitar. I listen to him, I know he's gonna be another Queenie. I also know if it wasn't for you maybe showing him up, he wouldn't be practicing like he does."

"Don't mention it," Junior said.

Shortly after that conversation, Mama and Uncle Dom decided, money being tight, that maybe the boys had enough of a foundation that they could develop their guitar skills on their own.

Sonny was ecstatic. Maybe now he could talk his old man into a trumpet.

Junior was ecstatic too.

Bread for Soup   2½ flour

6 tbsp of leaves   ½ cup (?) baking powder
6 eggs
½ tbsp. macaroni cheese
...
...
...

Grease cookie sheet.
(Read direct for (?))

6 (?) beat well
1 tbl (?) ...
½ cup grated mild cheese
½ cup fine bread crumbs
(?) cup of (?) ...
...with (?) ...
Baking powder   little pepper (?)

Mix altogether, put into (?)
pan grease well and bake (?) 15(?)
...
...

A Little White Square with Black Spots

I was damned. Going to Hell. Only eight years old and it had been determined already. My soul belonged forever and ever to Satan.

It was my First Communion day. I brushed my teeth that morning, so excited that I never considered the possibility of swallowing toothpaste and allowing something other than water into my stomach before I took Communion.

My sister Dolores and my cousins—Ange and Sonny and Georgie, and the other kids in the class at St. Francis, the Lithuanian church that stood right behind our house on Shehy—we had all been instructed by Miss Helen, our catechism teacher. Because none of us went to Catholic school we had to go to classes after Mass on Sundays, where Miss Helen quizzed us on the Ten Commandments and other such church things.

She went through them one by one, asking us to explain what each meant. When she got to "Thou shalt not commit Adultery," no one volunteered an answer. She fumbled to explain. We fidgeted.

Finally, Sonny blurted out, "Isn't that something like a burlesque show?"

"Close enough," she said and went on. Everyone was kind of snickering, but I doubt that Sonny's definition made it any clearer at all to any of us, including him.

Now it was the afternoon before our big day,

and Miss Helen ordered us to go straight home, speak as little as possible so we wouldn't commit adultery or any of those other sins, and go to bed early—long before midnight. After that **nothing but water** was permitted until after we got Communion at Mass on Sunday.

But out of habit that morning I mounded my brush with toothpaste, shoved it into my mouth, and scrubbed away. When I raised my eyes the face in the mirror told me what I had done. I spit, rinsed, spit, rinsed, spit, rinsed—till Dolores, in a strangely kind First Communion voice from outside the door, asked for me to please hurry and give someone else a chance at the bathroom.

Had I swallowed any toothpaste? Had there been any trace of it in the water that I was *sure* I swallowed? I tried to recall, but it was hopeless. The taste was there on my tongue in spite of the rinsing.

I've since learned the expression *scrupulous conscience*. I think I have one of those. I'm sure I had one when I was eight. If there was the slightest possibility that I had swallowed some toothpaste, then I had. How could I not have, since it was all mixed up there in the water that had been swishing around in my mouth?

That was settled. Now what should I do? Not make my First Communion? Unthinkable. My sister, my cousins, all the other classmates, my mother, my father, my family, the party we were having. No. I couldn't tell anyone. I would have to go through with it. And then I would burn in Hell for eternity.

A Little White Square with Black Spots

You see, that's the way I was. I had this crazy conscience that made me extra concerned about every little thing I did, but I also was too *proud*—another one of those big-time sins—to let anyone know that my conscience was torturing me. I was a mess.

Mama asked me if I was sick. I said no, and she didn't press it. She had enough other things on her mind, what with the First Communion and the feast she was preparing for afterwards.

When we were all dressed and inspected, we stopped next door for Georgie and then we all processed through the back yard, down Conti's driveway and over to the hall behind the church.

I was miserable. I would be struck by lightning, right through the stained glass window of the church on this sunny Sunday precisely at the moment the host touched my tongue. But the alternative would have brought unbearable shame upon me and I would still be among the living to feel it. I couldn't speak. I would say nothing, do nothing and just maybe God—Jesus—would take pity on me and allow me to spend my remaining years repenting and doing only good deeds, and finally He would consider all this against the toothpaste traces and the deception and take me in. I wanted to believe this but my conscience kept telling me I was doomed.

When Miss Helen lined us up in the church hall she asked for our attention. She told us how we were about to experience a communion with Our Lord unlike anything we had ever or would ever experience and we had to be spiritually ready. Our square little white souls had to be absolutely spotless. I pictured something like the negative of a domino. That was my soul, with one big black toothpaste spot right smack in the middle of it.

But, as so often happens in life, suddenly and from out of nowhere the hand of salvation fell upon me. It was in the form of Sonny, blurting out, "I brushed my teeth this morning!" He almost chuckled as he said it. He was not bothered at all. It was like a joke to him. "What if some toothpaste went down the tube?"

Miss Helen said, without hesitating, "Of course you brushed your teeth. I should hope all of you did." To which the others—all but me—nodded yes, of course.

"None of you *ate* the toothpaste. You just used it. That's no problem. Any other questions?"

Snatched from the jaws of Hell! I could have thrown my arms around Miss Helen and kissed her. I didn't of course. I just giggled with the others and we marched over towards the church.

That was the day I got my first reprieve.

And here I was four years later, an altar boy at the same church with my cousin Sonny. The scene was beyond the Communion rail now, into the sanctuary, right at the altar. And I was doomed again.

What happened was while Sonny and I were serving Mass this one Sunday, Father Sofranec, early in the Mass, took the hosts that he was going to use from a little wallet-like thing he called a burse then turned and handed it down to Sonny, kneeling at

A Little White Square with Black Spots

the altar step behind him, to carry into the sacristy. That's when the host must have fallen.

After Mass, when everyone else was gone and Sonny and I were just closing up to leave ourselves, I spotted it. A host, right there on the floor in the corner of the doorway between the sanctuary and the altar. Anyone could have stepped on it. Without thinking, I picked it up and set it on the dressing table in the sacristy.

Then it hit me. I had touched the host with my bare hand. Only a priest could do that.

Sonny hadn't seen me. Should I tell him? If I did we'd have to go over to the rectory and tell Father. I knew I had to do something. But, like always at these times, I couldn't.

At the door Sonny surveyed the sacristy. He saw it. "What's that host doing on the table?"

"What host?" I said. "Oh, that host."

"Where'd it come from?"

"Beats me."

"Now what do we do?" Sonny wasn't the kind to worry about details like I was, so his reaction surprised and disheartened me. If the host on the dressing table bothered him, even just a little bit, it was pretty serious.

I didn't answer.

"We can't touch it."

I was dying.

"We can't leave it there either. It's the body of Christ. Can't leave it lying around on the table."

"What happens," I said, "if we touch it?" I prayed maybe Sonny would have an out for me. Maybe he would say nothing happens. He was a year older than me and maybe he knew something I didn't know that would save me. And like I said, he didn't worry about the details the way I did. He would probably say, No harm done. We're only trying to help it by putting it away someplace.

What he did say was, "You go to Hell I think, unless you're a priest."

"Even if we just want to put it away?" I said. "To make it safe?"

"I ain't touching it, I know that."

If Sonny was scared to touch it, I was in really deep trouble. "I ain't either," I said.

"Guess we gotta go tell Father."

"But he's eating dinner now."

"He'll have to stop eating and come over and take care of this."

"He'll be mad. You know how he is about eating."

"It ain't our fault. I don't know how it got there."

"Me neither." I mumbled.

Which of course wasn't true. And here I was piling one sin on another. First I touch the host. Then I lie about it. Right there in the sacristy with the host staring me in the face. And I'd have to lie to Father, too. And I could never tell him the truth later in Confession. I'd have to carry this with me my whole life and die with this on my soul: I touched the body of Christ with my bare hand and then I lied about it right there in church in front of *it*.

Maybe if I become a priest, I thought. That might make it okay even if I wasn't a priest now when I touched it. It could maybe be retroactive.

But Sonny wasn't waiting around for me to decide I had a vocation. "Let's go tell Father."

"You go tell him," I said. "I'll run home and tell Mom why we're late for dinner.

"No you don't. If we're gonna interrupt his dinner, we do it together. "I didn't put that host there anymore than you did."

I wished he hadn't added that last part.

We crossed the driveway to the kitchen door of the rectory. Sonny knocked on the screen door. I stood back.

Father Sofranec appeared, a tall dark haired giant of a man, wiping his mouth with a napkin. "What is it?" he said. Nice guy that he was when you got to know him, he hardly ever smiled. Everything was serious to him. Sunday dinner was serious, and being interrupted was maybe more serious.

"Father," Sonny said. There's a host on the table in the sacristy. We don't know how it got there but we don't know what to do about it."

One of us knew, but I wasn't the one saying something untrue. I was thankful Sonny was there to do the talking.

"Is it just a host, a wafer?"

"Yeah, Father. Just the white host."

"Okay," he said. "It must have fallen out of the burse. It's okay. It wouldn't be consecrated." He wiped his mouth again with the napkin. "I'll take care of it when I go back over there. No problem."

Words of absolution from the pope himself couldn't have lifted the weight from my soul as well.

It's not consecrated. If it fell out of the burse, it didn't matter whether it landed on the table or the floor. It wasn't consecrated, which meant it wasn't the Body of Christ after all. Not yet. It was just a round piece of white stuff. Therefore, I could touch it. And the miracle was no one had to know I touched it. I hadn't committed a mortal sin, so I was saved from having to confess it and I was saved from the sin of not confessing it.

Father went back to his dinner and we went home to ours. I was suddenly starving for a plate of Mama's macaroni. And now it wouldn't go down like the last meal of a condemned man.

There was something scary about the thousands of rules in those childhood days, the things we had to worry about, the *venial* sins were bad enough. But what was really scary were those *mortal* sins that if we didn't confess and feel sorry for could send us to Hell where we'd stay forever and ever.

But at least the rules were clear.

Or were they?

There was that time, probably shortly after the host incident. We still lived on Rose Street. The war was over and new cars were once again being made. Father Sofranec always seemed to get the nicest things and get them first, because he came from a pretty rich family. It was hard to tell whether he enjoyed them because he didn't smile very much or show his pleasure the way I would have done if I had such neat things. But it was pretty obvious he

A Little White Square with Black Spots

was happy when he bought a new Buick. It was a long black streamlined model whose front fenders slanted all the way back across the doors into the back fenders. It was a real beauty.

One day Father asked me and Sonny to wash his car. It was a pleasure wiping the cloth along the sleek lines of this Buick. We'd have done it for nothing, but he paid us two bucks each, which made it that much more fun. Of course, we fought over the hose a little and both got pretty well drenched, even though Father stood there watching us, puffing on his pipe and now and then pointing out a spot we missed. You could tell he loved this car, even if he looked so serious. Sonny kind of hinted to me while we were horsing around that he wanted to squirt Father. But even Sonny wouldn't have done that. Father wasn't the kind of guy you squirt.

When we finished Father inspected our work and proclaimed it a good job. Then he asked us if we wanted to take a ride with him to visit some friends near Cleveland. We'd never pass up a chance to take a ride—a nice long ride all the way to Cleveland—in the new Buick. So we ran home to change and get permission and off we went.

Sonny and I agreed to take turns sitting up front. I got the back seat on the way there. Father drove like a maniac, but he was a priest, so I felt safe.

The ride was great. But I was nervous the whole visit. I never felt comfortable among strangers, so I remember fidgeting while we sat in the parlor of these friends of Father's, a nice middle-aged couple. They and Father chatted. They talked

Rose Street Revisited

about things that Sonny and I weren't too interested in, so we just sat and sipped our glasses of iced tea and tried to be polite. There wasn't much to add to this adult conversation anyway.

It got to be near suppertime and these folks asked Father to stay and eat. I wasn't too happy about this, and I don't think Sonny was either. It would be even more uncomfortable than just visiting. It was a Friday, so at home we were probably having macaroni *agli'olio* or with tuna fish sauce, both of which I loved, or maybe even some of Mama's pizza. I didn't like the idea of sitting in this strange house, nibbling at strange food and trying to eat with manners.

Then it got more uncomfortable than I could have imagined. Here it was, Friday, and the main course was ham, big thick slices of ham. It would be a mortal sin to eat it.

Of course I expected Father to refuse when the plate was passed and explain to these obviously non-Catholic friends that we'd go to Hell if we ate meat on Friday.

Instead, he took a slice. Then he passed it to Sonny who—even though I kicked him under the table—also took a slice.

I was appalled. How could they do this? Sonny passed the plate to me and I just passed it on to the lady of the house. Salad and the vegetables would be enough for me.

"Won't you have some ham?" she asked me, surprised.

"No thanks," I mumbled.

"Oh, I'm sorry. If you don't like it I can get

you something else."

"No, I'm fine." I looked across at Father at the same time Sonny kicked me back. Father frowned and shook his head at me. I shot a quick glance at Sonny. He grinned. He actually thought this was all very funny.

Well, I didn't care. My crazy cousin could sit there on a Friday and eat ham with a priest sitting right across from him and think it was a joke. The priest too! How could he? Eating meat right in front of two of his altar boys, and even being upset with me—I could tell by his expression—for not joining them. But I wouldn't do it. I was above all that. They could tempt me if they wanted. I wasn't going to get another one of those black marks on my soul even if they pinned me down and tried to stuff that ham down my throat!

The Mrs. apologized all over the place for being so unprepared. If she had known we were coming she would have had more to offer and all that. Father kept saying don't worry, that I hardly ever eat much any way—which wasn't true and he knew it, so he was adding a lie to his sin—and that I probably just wasn't hungry. The husband muttered a bit at his wife for not having more food on the table. Sonny kicked at me and grinned while he chomped on the ham.

As my embarrassment subsided, my sense of self-righteousness grew. Here I was, just a kid, but stronger than my cousin who was a year older, and stronger even than my priest in resisting the temptation to commit a mortal sin. It would be something I'd be proud of the rest of my life. But at the same time it was sad and disheartening that my priest, who was supposed to teach me to always do the right thing couldn't himself resist a mere piece of ham.

After dinner we hopped into the Buick and headed home. I settled into the soft leather of the front seat feeling pretty good about myself, and pretty scandalized over Father and Sonny.

Father drove home even faster than he drove there, but it was a long ride for me. Father was normally a man of few words, but as we pulled away from his friends' house, he carefully chose a few for me. "You didn't eat the ham."

"It's Friday, Father," I said.

"You noticed that I ate some."

I didn't respond.

"Why do you think I did?"

Was he apologizing to me? I tried to figure out where this was going. "I don't know, Father," I said. "You forgot it was Friday?"

I knew this wasn't true, but I thought maybe he wanted me to say that, to get him off the hook.

"I knew it was Friday."

Was he confessing to me? Was I the priest and he the sinner getting a sin off his shoulders? I couldn't think of anything to say.

"I knew as well as you that it was Friday." The big Buick was getting warm inside as we sped along a winding country road. I could feel Sonny grinning in the back seat.

"Do you remember," Father went on, "the story in the Bible about the time the scribes and the Pharisees accused Jesus of breaking the law because

he healed someone on a Sunday?"
"I guess I kind of remember," I said. I really didn't know much about the Bible since I never read it myself and only got bits and pieces of it at Mass, sometimes in Lithuanian, which I didn't understand at all. Even the English part I wasn't paying that much attention to. "Was he committing a sin?"
"There was a church law against it. Do you think he was committing a sin?'
"Jesus? I don't think so. Couldn't he kind of make his own rules?"
There was a loud guffaw in the back seat. Sonny was having fun, but I was really confused. I never heard Father talk so much about this kind of stuff to me. But what he was getting at was sinking in. I wasn't feeling so good anymore.
"Let's get back to the ham," Father said. "How do you think my friends felt about you not taking any?"
"I don't know. She thought I wasn't hungry. Or I didn't like ham or something."
"Whatever she thought, how do you think she felt about you sitting at her dinner table and just picking at side dishes."
"I guess—I don't know I guess she might have felt a little bad."
"You guess. How does your mother feel when someone sits at her table and doesn't eat?"
"She's Italian. That's different. She'd make them eat. And she wouldn't have meat today."
"That has nothing to do with it. How would she feel?"
"She'd feel bad," Sonny said before I could

say anything. I turned and glared at him. He smiled.

"Yeah," I said. She'd feel bad." I wanted him to know I got the point. "It's a sin to eat meat on Friday. It's a sin to make someone feel bad," I said. "What was I supposed to do?"

"What would Jesus have done?" Father asked.

It was a totally unfair question. There I was being the scribes and the Pharisees while Sonny in the back seat was being Jesus. It was totally unfair.

I didn't answer. I shriveled in the corner as close up to the door as I could get. I thought about my pure white square of a soul turning a pretty dinghy gray.

The rest of the trip Father became his usual quiet self, but he might as well have been preaching to me the whole way. His silence stung me as much as any more words would have. I could still feel Sonny grinning in the back seat. He had eaten ham on a Friday, and yet he and the priest had done the kind thing and were justified. I, on the other hand, had followed the rules and felt like a murderer.

When we got back to the rectory it was already dark. I was planning to punch Sonny on the walk through Conti's yard to our house, but before we took off Father asked us to wait. He went inside and came back out with an Isaly's Klondike ice cream bar for each of us. "Here," he said. "For the walk home."

I couldn't very well punch Sonny while we were eating a Klondike.

Now, so many years later, when I look back

I know that I must have been a real pain to be around the way I fussed so much about details. My definition of sin has narrowed pretty much to whatever I do that intentionally hurts someone else. I'm not sure that this makes life's choices any easier than in those childhood days, but it does sometimes make them different.

* * * * *

Dear Aunt Josephine

As Mother's Day approaches, I want to take this opportunity to mention a few things that I have been feeling in my heart these many years, but have never taken the time to tell you.

Everything I am that is good and decent I owe in great part to you Dear Lady and your wonderful family. My memories of the years that I lived with you on Rose Street and on Garland Avenue are so very dear to me and I'll remember them always.

You gave me shelter, you gave me guidance, you gave me religion and you gave me love and I have been able to pass these wonderful gifts on to my children as they will to theirs and on and on.

I haven't always shown my appreciation by being present at all the special occasions and family get-togethers but I assure you

that you have always been in my thoughts and also in my prayers.
I couldn't love you more if you were my Mother and you have been a Mother to so many but to none more than I and no one could love you more than I.
I'll always remember my Father's love for you and it made a lasting impression on me for I love Him and miss Him so.
To have a Happy Mothers Day precious Lady. I hope to see you soon.
Please don't ever forget me and remember always that I love you dearly.

        Yours alway
          Sonny

Transformation

How swift we settle into middle age:
This morning as I slowly swung from bed
And sat a moment on the edge, I tried
to clear my head a bit before I stood.
My eyes dropped slowly down toward my feet.
These must be someone else's feet, I thought.
They're much too old. Some eighty year old man
Came in last night and stole my feet from me
And left me his. The rest of me's the same.
It's just my feet, I wanted to believe.
I didn't dare to look into the mirror.
He might have taken more. So I just sat
And tried a little more to clear my head.
If anything besides my feet was gone
I didn't want to know. The mirror could wait.

To My Father
December 1980

As you, the old and ever gentle,
so ungently fall into the void
and tell through eyes already freed of sight
to me the fear and pain of leaving life,
I try to say my love to you in words.
But words, which seldom came to me in life,
cannot come now in death.
And so I simply watch and wait
until the moment you emerge,
again become my father, gentle man,
and gentle once again.

Gently Strumming

She holds the ukulele
like a mother nursing her child.
She bends her pretty face
and sings to it.

It coos back.

I watch and listen:
soft voice,
gentle strums,
halting,
feeling out the chords.

What's next? She looks up to ask
when nothing she tries works.

Try G, I say.

I don't really know what's next,
but G is clean, G is clear,
G moves sweetly higher,
almost fretlessly,
like her.

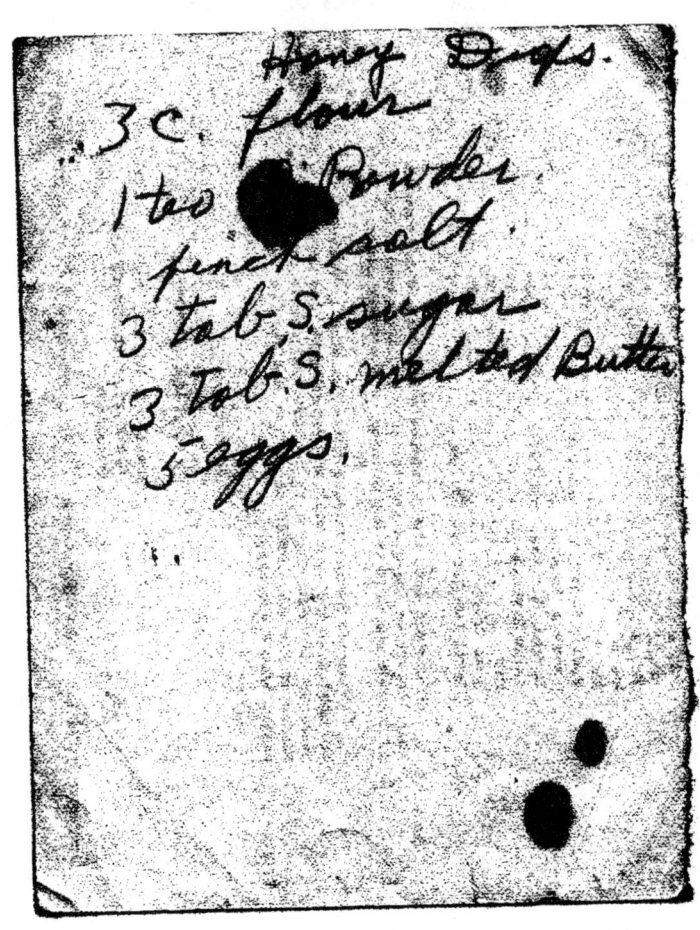

Honey Drops.

3 C. flour
1 tsp Powder.
pinch salt.
3 tabS. sugar
3 tabS. melted Butter
5 eggs.

Riddle

The literal-minded eat it for breakfast
and read its beautiful pictures
periodically.
The guru calls it a River.
T-shirts call it beach or bitch.
Sometimes we are told to get one.
It's tough and it sucks,
but every Christmas
if we're tuned in
Jimmy reminds us
it's a wonderful.

The Garland Girls

I think I can pinpoint the exact moment that I discovered girls. I don't mean mothers and sisters and aunts and cousins. I mean girls in the sense of *different from boys* and very, very appealing in some way that was different from macaroni or a good comic book or a movie or a donut. I couldn't begin to define the feeling, but I can recall it as if it was yesterday.

It was actually 1946 and I was eleven. We had just moved from Rose Street up the hill to 41 South Garland Avenue, and I would be switching to a new school, Lincoln, when school started up again in the fall. I was in the sixth grade.

You see, there weren't any girls on Rose Street. I mean there were girls, but in my mind they weren't *girls*. They were neighbors. They were friends of my sisters. We played kick the can and release the den and war and hide-n-go seek and hopscotch together. But I wasn't eleven yet so they weren't girls—yet.

But now, here I was. I was walking up the sidewalk toward our house. I didn't look where I was going, maybe because I couldn't see distances anyway since I needed glasses really bad, but I was the only one who knew this. I memorized the eye chart in the nurse's office at my old school, Roosevelt, so I could rattle off the letters even though I couldn't see even the big E. Why did I do this?. I was a skinny little guy who got A's without much effort and all I needed was glasses to make sure I would be forever separated from the *real* guys who lived in my old and now my new neighborhood.

So there I was, walking up the street towards my house, looking down at the cracked blocks of sidewalk, which was about all I could see pretty clearly. Suddenly there was a "beep beep" in the sweetest voice I'd ever heard. It was a sweet but distressed "beep beep" because a second later there she was, this girl on a bicycle screeching sideways right at me. She caught her balance and brushed by me. She almost fell, but she didn't look upset by this fact. She was close enough for me to see that. She glanced back over her shoulder and smiled and kept pedaling.

I'll always remember that smile, which was just one part of the prettiest face I had ever seen, the prettiest eyes, the prettiest nose, the prettiest hair. It was an epiphany, that vision. To this day I see that face and it speaks to me of all that is wonderful about life, about love, about innocence.

I found out later her name was Donna Jean. She was my age and in my class. She lived only four houses up the street. I was in love.

Luckily Donna Jean would never know this. It would have been a joke. In my mind every boy in the sixth grade, and the seventh and fifth too (if those little guys could even tell what a pretty girl was) had to be in love with Donna Jean. What chance could I possibly have?

I watched a blur of her turn into the back yard of our next door neighbors. Then another epiphany: a blurred bevy of beautiful girls suddenly appeared on the porch to greet her. I later learned that there were five young girls living there, no boys. One of them, Irene, who everyone called Inky, was also in my class at Lincoln.

One of the sisters called to someone across the street and my eye caught another blur of a girl leaning on her porch rail. Arlene she turned out to be, and also—would you believe it? —eleven years old and in my class.

As it turned out I was eventually to see these young ladies up close and verify their beauty. They were good friends with each other, in addition to a couple other classmates who lived on nearby blocks, another Donna Jean and a Janet. They liked to have parties—Halloween, birthday, any excuse would do—and I was one of the lucky guys who got invited regularly.

Why?

Simple. My cousin Sonny, who was also in my class, lived with me.

Now Sonny, as I saw it, was in some respects the male counterpart of Donna Jean of the bicycle. He was as suave, debonair, handsome, athletic—all those nice things—as I was not any of them. All these girls, in my eleven year old, educated, albeit blurry view, were in love with him. I was kind of along for the ride. I was Tonto to his Lone Ranger, Pancho to his Cisco Kid, Gabby Hayes to his Roy Rogers, maybe even Cheetah to his Tarzan.

But that was okay with me. He was my ticket to that wonderful sixth grade society.

As I said, this marked my discovery of girls. Not that I had any clear idea what they were for. All I could tell was it was a good feeling. If a girl talked to you, smiled at you, invited you to her parties where there were other girls who smiled at you and talked to you, it made you feel good. They didn't have to be your girlfriends or anything. They just made you feel good in a different way than you were used to feeling.

And sure, I know Sonny wasn't the only reason I was invited, but you know how it is when you're that age and you feel a little insecure?

Actually, the move to Garland was socially good in other ways too. I suddenly found myself with a lot of school friends. Guys, I mean. They'd come to the house and sit around on my porch and usually want to play catch in my driveway.

Come to think of it, it was usually when the Garland girls were out and about, sitting on their porches or riding their bikes up and down the block.

And also come to think of it, these guys usually wanted to be on the street end of the driveway while we tossed the ball, where the Garland girls could watch them perform.

Do you think I'm being a little paranoid about this? Is my vision still blurred?

Maybe when we have our fiftieth class reunion a couple years from now I'll creak over to one of the Donna Jeans or to Inky and ask a few questions.

But do I really want to know?

A couple years after we moved to Garland, when we went to eighth grade at East High School, I flunked my first algebra test. Miss Hadley put her tests on the board and Anna Nespeca, who had always sat directly behind me at Lincoln, didn't take algebra, so she wasn't there to whisper to me what was on the board. I finally had to tell my mother I needed glasses.

I've worn glasses ever since. I can see clearly now. But when I look back through all those years, so many things are still blurred.

One thing that isn't blurred is a beautiful face that becomes all the faces of all those Garland girls who were in my life back then. It smiles forever and makes me feel forever good.

Love Notes From Teresa

How many times a note clipped in my briefcase
makes my day:
"I love you Daddy very very much,"
a smile face, and "Teresa."
A simple sentence lettered by a child
and placed discreetly where I had to see
first thing upon the opening of the case.
Or sometimes placed within a book
or in a lunch bag,
or hanging from the string to close the closet light.

But you are only ten.
And what of notes when you are seventeen?
When I am sometimes not so sure
and need a sign or two?

How will the hinges creak on briefcase then,
and I left looking into blackness,
books and papers, notes I write myself
to tell myself to not forget
something or other that I have to do,
someone to call, someone to see,
someone to send a memo to?

Where will we be Teresa then?
On what note will you leave me for the world
and come back just for Sunday dinners now and
then
and call me Grandpa to instruct your child?

Help me Teresa to hold on to simple days
by holding on yourself.
And now and then
leave me a note to tell me of your love.

* * * * *

Rose Street Revisited

The following is an account of an adventure that occurred eons after those Rose Street days, after I had become a father and a grandfather many times over. I include it because it brings us full circle, back to the place where it all began for the Leone family and yet to a world that is so different that it might as well be another planet in another galaxy. Who, I ask, are the aliens in this story?

Four Americanos and a French Bride

When you have three sons heading for Europe—and when one of them's Dan so you know he'll rub off on the other two, and when the other two are Gene (who for reasons beyond me speaks Italian and French and is personal friends with all but two or three citizens of both France and Italy) and Chris (who when he's not being his silent self is sometimes Dan and sometimes Gene)—you *don't* decide to tag along. Not if you're me and your idea of adventure is stepping out on the porch before leaving for work to see whether you'll need a sweater or a light jacket.

Unless you take leave of five or six of your senses, like I did.

Of course you fly "stand-by." That's the system where you save a hundred dollars in exchange for no less than three years lopped off your life expectancy. It means you leave from different American cities on different days and some of you end up in London and some in Paris and some in Hamburg, Germany and you all plan to meet at the railroad station in Marseilles at some time and day not clearly specified.

I attach myself (literally) to Chris, the youngest and therefore the sanest of the three. We draw Hamburg.

Well, by some miracle (not one to take unnecessary chances, I had my aunts recite among them 1450 rosaries and make twenty-one novenas) we do meet, more or less, at the railroad station in Marseilles.

I won't bore you with our French adventures, except to say that they involved a wedding, an octopus, a bevy of topless beach beauties, and dangling from a rock several thousand feet above sea level. I don't mean that in a "says so on this map" sense. I mean clutching a rock and kicking air and looking down and seeing foaming water way way down there.

But, as I say, that's another story (or so). We'll skip to the Italy part.

As might be expected (Gene being among us), the pretty, young French bride (see "wedding" above), decides to accompany us to Italy *without her groom*. She's never seen it and her new husband can't take the time off work this month. They'll honeymoon next month. So, if it's all right with us...

Of course it's all right with us. There's

something about brides at the moment of their bridedom that you don't argue with them. Whatever they say, whether in American or French, they are right. When they happen to be beautiful *and* French *and* brides and you're my three sons, even if they're newly married to your good French friend, you don't object.

As for my own feelings on the matter: 1) I was still in trauma from the flight and therefore without respected opinions, 2) I had not learned enough French to know whether they were discussing "taking the bride to Italy with us" or "handing a pen to someone's aunt at the train depot," and 3) I may be a lot older than my sons, but the imagination still functions as well as the youngest of them and—having recklessly decided to tag along—I was game for anything. I was intrigued by the idea of trying to explain to our Italian cousins how we came to have a newly married yet groomless French girl as our travelling companion. How would that possibly translate?

So Madame Fabienne Couturier bids a fond farewell to her husband of two days and joins three young Americanos and their father in Marseilles, where we pick up a basic Renault at the car rental and speed off toward Italy.

Let me tell you about our basic Renault. It is basic. One can not drive around Europe with American sized cars. Nor, with the price of gasoline, can one afford all the power luxuries. It is a subcompact two-door with no air conditioning, no radio, and certainly no space for the bodies and luggage and camping equipment of five people spending two weeks in Italy. But with Gene anything is possible. He performs a miracle that rivals that of the loaves and fish. Every piece of our luggage and ourselves, not necessarily in familiar patterns, actually makes it inside *le car*.

Now age has its advantages. It entitles one to the respect of the young. It also allows one to be a big baby with impunity. I refuse to take a turn driving on this unfamiliar continent. In return I am happy to volunteer for permanent back seat duty.

There is actually room for only two in the back, but remember, we are five, and with two bucket seats up front, someone has to draw the back middle. Fortunately, Fabienne is a *tiny* French bride and my three boys are still young enough to be slim. So we back-seaters—usually Fabienne, one of the boys and I— do fit. It's just that it is a *perfect* fit. No movement is possible except perhaps for the lower arms. If we wish to applaud the maneuverings of the driver we have to do so by slapping our palms together vertically.

It's July, so of course it's hot—unbearably so at those frequent times on the highway when traffic is backed up. The crowded, narrow streets of the cities are even worse. We bake as we weave our way in and out of the traffic, both pedestrian and vehicular, on the narrow stones of the cities, sometimes giving a nudge to little old ladies with large shopping bags extending to the ground from either arm. They seem not to care, but instead welcome us with strange operatic arias that they warble off-key to the back of our Renault.

Fabienne, fortunately, is a good sport about everything. She stoically accepts the bad accommodations, takes her turns driving, and translates into French for us when the boys and I can't understand each other's English.

She also has a great command of English. The fact that she speaks it with a French accent makes it even better and somehow more grammatical and polished.

It is embarrassing for me to discover that she can speak our language so fluently. Granted it was a long time ago, but after two years of high school and one of college French, I now discover that the one sentence I recall *(Comment allez vous aujourduis)* isn't even the way you're supposed to say whatever it means in the first place.

Anyway, we five are off from Marseilles for Italy.

Our first stop before crossing the Italian border is in the French Alps, where the bride's new sister-in-law lives with her family. They feed us and put us up for the night.

The next day my boys climb rocks with our Alpine friends. Fabienne and I stay down on solid ground never looking up and wondering in our different languages what would possess sane (Ha!) human beings to play such games with gravity. They descend, we're told (for we can't look) by bouncing off the side of the mountain while dangling from ropes until they get right back where they started, on solid ground next to Fabienne and me. Not a bit of forward progress but we are relieved and they seem happier for the experience. After a hearty meal we set off in our matchbox car for the border.

    Our first Italian destination: Florence, where my nephew Marco and his wife Adrianna show us the wonders of the city at night and we treat them to a many-course Italian dinner at one of Florence's fine establishments. The extensive menu makes sense to only two of the seven of us, so the owner, after trying to explain the choices to blank faces, makes a reasonable suggestion. He will bring us all some of everything.

    This we happily agree to and before long the most delicious Italian delicacies begin to appear. Dan, a restaurant reviewer by trade thinks he had died and gone to heaven. If you are familiar with low budget but critically acclaimed films, think *The Big Night*. Think *Babette's Feast* (even if it's French).

    Then the bill comes. Think *the Poseidon Adventure*.

    I have no idea what the exchange rate is, but I have just charged on my credit card a figure that has more zeroes than the scoreboard in a no-hit game. Fortunately, Fabienne is able to explain to me that there are about six million Italian *liras* to an American dollar, so I get up off the floor and we bid farewell to our Florentines and speed off for Rome.

    But it is impossible to reach Rome until the next day, and we are too tired to drive through the night, so Gene finds a secluded mountain road where we can camp. A few hundred feet up the mountain he pulls off the road and the guys pitch a tent. The tent will accommodate four, but I voice a fear of bears and Fabienne voices a fear of something called "ours," so we two elect to sleep in the car.

Like a gentleman, I give Fabienne the comfort of the backseat, all three and a half by two feet of it. Up front the steering wheel and the gearshift prevent my stretching out, so I am confined to one of the buckets. Neither bears nor "ours" approach during the night. I know for a fact. I haven't slept.

But mercifully the morning breaks and we are on our way once again.

Around noon we arrive in Rome at my cousin Carmela's apartment, where she has prepared a feast to rival our Florentine one. We have a hearty seventy-two-course meal with pasta somewhere around the center.

Now back home in the states, in our many-peopled house, we were used to simply putting all the food out at once on the huge lazy Susan that centered our round dining room table. We would eat and spin, eat and spin, until everyone was full. No one kept track of courses.

Here in Italy, the first course, an anti pasto, is the only thing on the table. Poor Dan and Chris have not mastered the art of saving room for later courses, so they dive for seconds and thirds with the encouragement of Cousin Carmela. Then the food is cleared to make room for the next course. This process repeats and repeats itself until finally

several varieties of cheeses and fruit are placed before glazed eyes.
"Mangia! Mangia!" Carmela insists. How could we not oblige? Needless to say, we need naps before we can start on our walking trip down to *il coliseo*, which turns out to be the Coliseum.
How strange that from my cousin's apartment we could take a stroll downtown to see the Coliseum, and then mosey over to Saint Peter's Basilica and the Sistine Chapel, and wave up to the Pope at Vatican City. By the time we returned to Carmela's, hours and many aching feet later, what do we find waiting for us? Of course, another feast of many courses.

After an overnight stay, we follow Carmela's son Stefano and his wife Elena east to the Apennines and the village of Barrea, where my father was born and spent the first fourteen years of his life.
Through good fortune, Carmela owns the old family home in Barrea. My boys, Fabienne, and my Italian cousins are very patient with me as I blubber around the family home and then the village and the woods where my father had his childhood. Everything, absolutely everything, is sacred to me.
Stefano and Elena have to return to work in Rome, but they leave us the key to the house in Barrea, so we can savor the place.
From Barrea we make a short trip over to Pietrabbondante, my mother's hometown, and a longer trip south to Cassino, then to Naples, and as far south as Calabria. Then we return to Barrea

for a couple more days before driving back to Rome.

From Rome, Dan flies back to San Francisco, Chris, Gene, and I fly back to Ohio and Fabienne drives our rental back to Marseilles where her new husband picks her up.

We three Americanos have traveled the country for two weeks with this French bride-sans-groom in the most cramped conditions imaginable. She never complains, never tries to impose her opinions on us. Instead, she often smiles and says stupide, which sounds very much like the English word "stupid," but, I am told by one of my sons, translates to "full of wonder, wonderful."

Rose Street Revisited

Buona Sera: To Danny

Danny, when I was a child,
your namesake uncle and your grandpa
would sit on summer evenings sipping wine
and talk a language comfortable to them.

I would be there too.

When parting time approached they said their *buona
    seras.*
Perhaps a dozen interrupted further dialogue.
They didn't want to part.

How bored I was!
A child who could not know the meaning of such
    sounds
interrupted only by the wine,
a child who sat and tried in vain
to like the bitter bit of wine that sparkled in his glass.

Yet now I know what way back then there was
    that now is lost,
what brothers meant to one another,
how a simple love was breathed in every syllable
and consecrated with the wine.

If ever man was like my father, Danny was.
I loved him for that, though I didn't understand.

Danny, if you would please your father, learn from
    them:

Buona Sera: To Danny

Don't be lost in this day's world
where self-survival, self-indulgence reign,
but turn to brothers, offering the wine,
saying—if they understand or not—your love.
Live with them in such a way
That *buona seras* simply interrupt a dialogue.

Rose Street Revisited

DOCUMENTS

P. 5 **Cranberry Salada**
This was and still is a favorite holiday treat, especially with turkey on Thanksgiving. It pretty much replaced the traditional cooked cranberries in our family. Notice the reference to "ice box." On Rose Street that's what we had. When we moved to Garland we got a refrigerator.

P. 9 **Rose Street Boys**
This picture shows five of the "boys" (as servicemen were called during World War II) from five of the families on Rose Street. In mid-war the local newspaper ran a photograph of the street headlined "Block-Long Rose St. Sends 22 Men into Army, Navy." An accompanying article was titled "22 Stars for 32 families—That's Rose Street's Role in War." Before the war ended two years later there were over thirty men and a woman from those 32 families serving in the war.

P. 17 **Lemon Drop Cookies**
This recipe is in Mama's writing. When a family wedding is approaching, my kids still make arrangements with Aunt Georgina to meet at her place and make a few batches.

Documents

P. 20 Rose Street Ladies
Left to right are Mary (Mary the Green House) Vagnarelli, Delia Febo, and Cecilia (Donna Chi' chill) Palumbo.

P. 26 Aunt Mary's Easter Bread
A number of variations on Easter Bread circulated in handwritten recipes among the family and neighbors.

P. 36 Toots with the Gretsch
Couldn't find a snapshot with Sonny playing his first guitar, the Gretsch that he passed along to me when Uncle Dom bought him a new one. This is my brother Toots playing it several years after we moved from Rose Street to Garland Avenue. I still own and treasure it.

P. 45 Young Ladies Sodality
At Saint Francis of Assisi Parish every spring a May crowning was held. The Young Ladies' Sodality selected one of its members to crown the Blessed Mother in a ceremony with all the other girls in attendance.
In the background on the left is our family house at 846 Rose Street.

P. 49 Grocery List
Mama would send Dolores or me over to Conti's grocery store almost daily with a list like this that Mrs. Conti would fill in and then put on our bill.

Rose Street Revisited

P. 55 (and Front Cover)   Rose Street Kids
Something special was going on because we normally didn't dress like this. That's Dolores, me, and Georgie front row left. Further along is Angelo and on the right end is Sonny.

P. 70   The Dukes
These are the founders of the *Duca degli Abruzzi* (The Duke's). My Grandpa, Beatangelo Vitullo, is the first gentleman on the left, front row.

P. 82   Bread for Soup (Cheesies)
This is a messy copy in Mama's writing, obviously often used. Cut to the size of croutons, these are intended to be added to wedding soup, but make a delicious snack on their own right, a problem for the cook, since everyone who walks through the kitchen wants a couple to taste.

PP. 97-98   A Letter From Sonny
While I was working on *Rose Street* I searched in vain for a letter I remembered my cousin Sonny writing to my mother sometime after my father died in January 1981. Recently my sister-in-law Louise, searching for something else, came across this letter. There's no date, but it was written for Mother's Day.

Documents

P. 102 Honey Drop Cookies

Of the special cookies of my childhood on Rose Street, honey drops rank number one. Don't be fooled by Mama's brief recipe. These are tough cookies to make. The missing part: "Mix well. Roll into strips. Cut in small pieces. Cook on stove in hot oil until golden brown. Place in bowl. When cooled, pour honey over and mix well. Form in ring or flat pan."

There's a very sad story to tell about honey drops: It was the day before Christmas Eve in 1964. Aunt Mary still lived on Rose Street. Two of her brothers had died that fall, and she was in mourning. She complained to Mama that she didn't have a single cookie to serve, so Mama gave her a bowl of honey drop "noodles" that she had been working on. Aunt Mary could finish them.

That night Aunt Mary worked on the honey drops while she and Mama talked on the phone. My father, after a heart attack, was getting out of the hospital the next day, so this picked up their spirits, but, Aunt Mary told Mama, she was exhausted from the tedious job of finishing the honey drops. When the conversation ended, Aunt Mary sat on her couch to rest. She never woke up. Mama was devastated. Aunt Mary had been her strength through all the years when they were next door neighbors on Rose Street.

Of course, Mama blamed the honey drops for wearing out Aunt Mary. It was years before she could bring herself to make them again.

P. 109 The Febo Family

The Febos lived two houses up from Aunt Mary and us on Rose Street. The fact that our family had this portrait as well as First Communion pictures of the Febo kids says something about how close neighbors were back then.

When we moved from Rose Street, the Febos bought our house. To this day, the youngest child, Loretta, lives there with her family.

Mrs. Febo, Delia, was the one in the neighborhood who was called on to pray over any of us who were victims of the *mal occhia,* the "evil eye." She dipped her tiny finger over and over into a dish with a mixture of garlic and oil and made the sign of the cross on strategic parts of our ailing bodies. It was enough to keep us kids from complaining of sickness.

Many years later, when Delia was in her nineties, she walked each morning down Rose Street and up Wilson to attend daily Mass at St. Stephen's Church, even though the house was right behind the church. Father Bonnot, the pastor there, had a gate placed directly across from the house and gave Delia a key.

Documents

P. 111 Uncle Dom and Grandpa Beatangelo
This photo was taken in 1941 after a family wedding dinner at the hall behind St. Francis Church. Uncle Dom, on the left with loosened tie, dangles his perpetual cigarette. If they were turned just a little to their left, they would be facing the back of our house on Rose Street.

P. 121   What Could We Get into Next?
Susan and Jeff, two of Aunt Mary DeMaria's grandchildren, sit on the porch step of her Rose Street home, taking a break during a tough day of play.

Back Cover   Some of Us at 846 Rose Street
Mama wrote "Our Gang Comedy" on the back of this snapshot, taken at the front porch probably in 1942 or '43. This must have been a special day because I'm wearing a suit. I'm at the front next to Papa, who's holding my sister Dolly's daughter, Marion. Behind me, up on the porch, is my sister Rita, holding Aunt Jessie's son, Jimmy. Mama and Aunt Lena are at the very back. In front of them are my sister Dolores, Aunt Jessie, and my sister Dolly.

129

ABOUT THE AUTHOR

"To prove that I didn't make up the guitar story," Carmen says, "Here I am with my first guitar posing on the front walk at 846 Rose Street."

Carmen is retired from his position as Associate Professor of English at Edinboro University of Pennsylvania, but teaches part-time at Youngstown State University. He's still called Junior by some of the old Rose Street gang.

The father of eleven children and even more grandchildren, Carmen has had numerous stories, poems, cartoons, and articles published. He also plays guitar in a local band. This is his second book.

Rose Street is available at various bookshops throughout the country or through the Internet.

For more information or to contact the authors, please write to:

Culcagni and Associates
5922 South Avenue, Suite C
Boardman, Ohio 44512
(330) 965-9765
(330) 758-0014 fax
E-mail: racalcagni@gateway.net